DARK
TERRITORIES

DARK TERRITORIES

Cover illustration and design by Steven Gilberts.
Cover art © 2007 by Steven Gilberts.
Cover Layout by Neal Levin
Interior Layout by Mary SanGiovanni, Gary Frank & Nanci Kalanta

ISBN (10): 0-9792346-2-X
ISBN (13): 978-0-9792346-2-0
Printed in the United States of America.
10 9 8 7 6 5 4 3 2 1
HW Press for GSHW Press
Website: http://gshw.net

Printed in the United States

DARK TERRITORIES

Edited by

Gary Frank
and
Mary SanGiovanni

HW Press
Fair Lawn, NJ

DEDICATION

This book is dedicated in fond and affectionate memory to Charles Grant - a scholar, a gentleman, a thinker, a man of wit and a man of vision, an incredible writer, and a very much missed friend.

ACKNOWLEDGMENTS

The editors would like to thank:
Harrison Howe and Michael Penncavage, for their help with the ins and outs of anthology publishing.
Nanci Kalanta for helping with interior layouts.
Neal Levin for helping with getting the cover file together
Ellen Datlow, for her advice.
The GSHW board, past and present, and the GSHW membership, for their patience and support, and for their enthusiastic faith in the anthology series.
Pat Graversen and the original, founding members of the Garden State Horror Writers for having the vision to create an organization to help those who believe dark fiction and horror are credible, important fiction genres.
The contributors, for writing such quality stories, and for really making this book something both editors are extremely proud of. Your talent continues to honor and strengthen the Garden State Horror Writers as a whole.

CONTENTS

Foreword
By Gary Frank

Welcome to the new anthology from the Garden State Horror Writers, Dark Territories. Come in. Sit down. Forget what you know about "horror" and all the tropes, clichés and movies you've seen because what you're about to experience goes beyond all that. There are no hockey-masked slashers or serial killers stalking people in their dreams. Oh no. These stories are something different. They wander into darker realms of the human spirit, exploring what it means to be human. Sometimes the truth is illuminated, sometimes darkness is the victor, because that's what being human is about.

It's easy to brush off horror as all gore and scare, but the authors of these stories know there is much more to the subject than just that. They understand dread and terror, consequences and what makes a person do a thing that most of us consider evil. These writers understand what becomes of people when their environment controls them and what they'll do to take back that control. This is the exploration of human nature.

That's why we write horror. Oh sure, we write because we enjoy a good scare, but underneath the blood, guts, and paralyzing terror, is a snapshot of the human spirit struggling against extraordinary circumstances. That's what these authors, most members of the Garden State Horror Writers, understand. Being human, sometimes we do the right thing and sometimes we don't, but we always *believe* we're doing right and in that believing, we occasionally do bad things for the right reasons.

I'm very proud of this collection of stories (twelve new and three reprints) the people who wrote them, and the GSHW as a whole. It's a good bunch of folk who represent the Garden State as writers of science fiction, fantasy, and horror. I'm very grateful to the group for all they've given me and also for the opportunity to edit this anthology.

To all of you reading this anthology, thanks for stopping by and visiting with us for a while. It's my hope that when you leave, these stories stay with you and give you something to think about, whether it's second chances, missed opportunities, love, hate, or what it means to be human.

Thank you and good night.

Gary Frank
March, 2008

Foreword

By Mary SanGiovanni

I think, as a species, we're territorial. We're habitually territorial. We choose the same seat on the bus or train, the same spot in our local favorite diner or restaurant, the same "assigned seat" in a classroom, long after we outgrow the years where assigned seating promoted order. We protect what's ours. We defend what little patches of earth and glass and cement we're given in this world, and we do so without even thinking about it. Well, not too much.

But there are inside places, too — places in our heads, places in our hearts — where we are just as protective, just as territorial. We protect our feelings, our beliefs, our thoughts. We protect our memories. We protect our dreams and fantasies. We're territorial. We own those places in our heads, and all the intangibles in them.

Maybe more than any of those things, I believe we're territorial about our fear. Whether it's simply a fact that we don't want others laughing at us, or whether the fear is such that its dimensions are too awful to fully consider in the daylight of our conscious thought, we harbor our fears in secret places and shove them down into dark and forgotten corners, tucked away from the landscape of our minds. But they're still there, those fears, marking off dangerous back alleys and wild, terrible, overgrown weeded lots.

I think many people believe writers are territorial, too. Maybe more so than anyone else, scribbling away at mad hours, shutting out family and friends during the process of creation, blowing off social obligations, hiding away while all the secret things they want to say come pouring out in a work which is theirs all theirs, thank-God-for-copyrights, all theirs. I don't know about that assessment, though. Because writers share eventually, see. By virtue of exploring conflict, of developing character and weaving atmosphere and constructing plot, they become master or mistress of their territories of fear. They conquer those wild lands, stick a flag in them, and claim those territories as their own. But they also let you tour through. They don't promise nothing will nip at your heels, but they let you walk through.

Assembled in this book are some of the finest stories I've ever seen the members of the Garden State Horror Writers produce. From new members to veterans of all different experience levels and backgrounds, we have stories of hate, regret, lust, dread, love, vengeance, honor, terror, wonder, and good old-fashioned fear. We're allowed a peek into the territories of the human heart, the human mind, where few are allowed to go, and fewer are allowed to return from unscathed. Each of these stories was chosen because to Gary and I, as editors, they were parcels of unsettling fiction we were proud to annex into our dark territory. Each one captured what we felt horror was really about — not the creepy thing that goes bump in the night, but the often primal, instinctive, and very often chilling way in which we react to it — in which we protect the territory of our sanity and security.

These writers have captured the simple aspect of humanity that at heart, we're territorial — creatures of habit. And some of those habits are bad....

On behalf of Gary and myself, we thank you for coming to visit. We hope you manage to find your way out okay. This territory is still mostly untamed, and we're not sure what might follow you out, back into the lands you call your own, the lands you call safe. And while we're sad to see you go, we're content to let the dark swallow up the gate behind you. We're content to go back to the dens and warrens and caves which belong to us.

They're ours, after all, all ours.

Mary SanGiovanni
The darkest territory of New Jersey
March, 2008

Dream Girl
John R. Platt

John R. Platt has published more than 50 stories in anthologies and magazines around the world. He served three terms as President of the Garden State Horror Writers, and edited the first GSHW anthology, Jersey Ghouls. John moved to Maine in 2006, where he works as a freelance writer and marketing consultant.

*A*nne-Marie O'Connor has always been the girl of my dreams.

From the pale freckles across the paler skin of her face to the way her eyes crinkled when she smiled at me, from the soft whisper of her voice to the curve of her hips and chest, every detail seemed created exactly for me.

It's been almost twenty-five years since the first time I saw Anne-Marie. And just a few minutes since I saw her last. She's changed, grown up, become a woman, but I still see her exactly the same way I did when we were seventeen and in love.

I wonder how much I have grown up in days and years since.

And I wonder how things might have been different.

We grew up just a few streets from each other, not that we knew it at the time. Freehold's school districting lines made sure that we didn't meet until sixth grade. Even then, I only saw her a few times a year, when our classes got together for big field trips. We'd visit Monmouth Battlefield, the cookie factory in nearby Englishtown, or a music concert by some local classical group. I'd get a glimpse of her in the crowd, her red hair shining in the sun, but I never approached her. Not then. It was two years before I even knew her name.

That didn't stop me from thinking about her. I asked around, found out who she was, but I never had the courage to do more. I dreamed of a thousand conversations before we ever actually spoke.

High school brought us closer, if slowly. We didn't talk much in those awkward freshman and sophomore days, but we did share a few classes, and worked on the occasional school spirit project together. Her dad started selling Buicks at my dad's dealership, and then her family moved to the old Porter house on the next block. Mom and Dad invited her whole family to barbeques every few months.

I dreaded and dreamed about those picnics for weeks before-hand. Anne-Marie would walk into our yard, lagging a few steps behind her parents. I'd walk over to her as quickly as I could get my legs to work. We'd smile and make small talk, then disappear from the adults for a while to sneak a smoke, or go for a swim in the pool.

Being away from our classmates and cliques gave us the freedom to talk to each other. In the months between parties, we barely spoke.

Anne-Marie was one of the prettiest girls in our class. As such, we moved in different circles. She dated here and there. I just sat on the sidelines. Waiting. And dreaming.

But in our Senior year, something between us finally clicked, and my daylight hours were filled with as much of her as I saw in my dreams. We talked for hours — more than I'd ever talked to anyone else — and made out for longer. And a few nights in the back of her dad's Buick, she helped me understand how much more to life there is than dreams.

It didn't last. Some stupid argument one night after a movie and it was all over as suddenly as it had begun. I wish I could say I didn't remember what the fight was about, but truth is, it was petty, stupid, and I don't even want to acknowledge it.

Anne-Marie went to the Prom with Stan Olmsted. Angry, hurt, and a more than a little bit lost, I went with Sally Burns. Afterwards, Sally and I had awkward sex at a noisy, beer-filled party.

Anne-Marie found out, of course. There are no secrets in high school. We walked past each other in the hall on Monday, and the way she looked at me... Her face was blank, but her blue eyes were a combination of sad and angry that I'd never seen before. It struck me dumb, and I couldn't say a word to her. Hell, I could barely meet her tearful stare.

For months after that, I tried to dream about her smiling eyes again, but all that ever came to me was that look.

I don't think we ever spoke again after Prom night. Graduation was just a few weeks away. Then came summer jobs, and after that we were off to college in different parts of the country.

I found new friends, new interests, new girlfriends. But I never stopped thinking about her. Dreaming about her.

Oh, I'd hear things once in a while, from my mom and dad, or through the old-boy high-school alumni network. Mr. O'Connor died the summer after college graduation. Heart attack. Mrs. O'Connor moved away and remarried. Anne-Marie got a job in California selling pharmaceuticals.

Beyond that, I lost track.

For me, college brought out my creative side, and I switched my major from business administration to fine arts. My dad did not approve, wanted me to take over the dealership when he retired. Instead, I found myself a career in advertising soon after graduation. I bounced around for a few years, from small agency to less-small agency. Then, on my thirtieth birthday, I landed in Chicago with an Art Director position at a fairly prestigious firm. They joked at the number of red-haired models in my portfolio, but hired me anyway. Thank god.

A few years ago, I met Sara, a dark-haired beauty and a hell of a copywriter. She didn't exactly make my heart sing, but with her, I felt more comfortable than I ever had with anyone else, if that makes sense. We settled down, got married, and bought a little brownstone to call our home.

And yet through it all, I never went a month without pulling the old Patriots yearbook down from the shelf, flipping through it to look at my dream girl's picture.

I still dreamed about Anne-Marie, and occasionally, I thought about her during sex. Sara never seemed to notice.

I wonder if she has noticed that I never came to bed tonight?

All this time, Anne-Marie had been living just a few miles away, in a suburb called Addison, west of the city. She looks as stunning as ever. The news video is out of focus at times, but mostly is shows her in crystal clarity.

A few wrinkles around her eyes and at the corners of her mouth are the only sign of the passage of years. But her face is a mask. Blank, with eyes a combination of sad and angry that I know so well.

Anne-Marie holds her head up proudly as two uniformed officers escort her out of her home, into a waiting squad car.

Then the image cuts to the gurneys being led out of the house. Three bodies, sheets covering their faces in white anonymity.

The murders were the lead story on the 10 o'clock news. I haven't moved from in front of the TV since. I've seen the footage again on every channel, on the late-night local news re-runs. And an hour or so ago, the story hit CNN and Fox.

I'm sure this morning's *Tribune* will have it as their lead headline, if I can ever get out the door to pick up the paper.

Outside my windows, the rising sun is beginning to reflect off the waters of Lake Michigan. Sara's alarm clock will go off in a few minutes. I have to leave for work in an hour. There's no way I can handle it. I'll tell Sara I'm sick, call out of work. Finally go to bed.

But I'm afraid. Afraid to sleep, afraid to close my eyes for too long. Afraid to dream.

When I finally drift off, which Anne-Marie will greet me in my dreams? Will it be the smiling girl I've dreamed of for so long? The one with the hurt and angry eyes? Or the one I saw tonight?

I'm afraid to know the answer.

What inspired "Dream Girl"?

The inspiration behind "Dream Girl" — I try not to have regrets, but every once in a while, I wonder what happened to the people who used to be in my life. Where are they now? Who are they? Have they changed, or are they still the same people that I once knew or loved? Are they better off without me, or worse? Did I ever really know them to begin with? I ask myself these questions, but I don't go looking for answers, except in stories like "Dream Girl."

Forty-Nine Cents
Dan Foley

Dan Foley lives in Connecticut with his wife Tere. Dan has worn many hats in professional life, including Sailor, Licensed Senior Reactor Operator, Nuclear Operations Consultant, Insurance Agent, and, once again, Nuclear Operations Consultant. He developed his rather dark sense of humor while serving on nuclear submarines. Dan started writing late in life, publishing his first short story at the age of fifty-seven. His stories have appeared in Maelstrom 1, Dark Notes From NJ, Nocturne Magazine, Wicked Karnival, and Hellbound Book's Damned Nation, and DeathGrip: Exit Laughing to name a few. Dan has three daughters, all of whom enjoy a good horror tale. His four grandchildren are not old enough to read his stories... yet.

I don't know when I started getting these little blasts from the past, but I'm pretty sure the first one was in early June. There might have been earlier ones, but I didn't notice them. But the one in June, that one got my attention. I reached in the right hand pocket of my jeans to get something, I don't even remember what is was, and I felt something sharp bite into my middle finger. "Damn!" I swore as I yanked my hand out of the pocket and examined my finger, fully expecting to see a drop of blood at its tip. When all I saw was a red spot, I carefully dipped the hand back in the pocket to see what the hell I had in there.

What I found was a bottle cap – a bottle cap that had no right being there. I knew what it was, and that there was something weird about it as soon as my fingers had a hold of it. It was bent like it had been popped off with a can opener and I could feel the cork seal under the lid. For some reason, that little bit of tactile information sent off alarm bells in my head. When I took it out and turned it over in my hand my entire world went crazy.

In my hand (it had to be my hand, didn't it?) was an old White Rock cap from a Black Cherry soda. The nymph was there, wings and all, dressed in her diaphanous gown and staring at her reflection in the pool. Out of habit, I brought the cap close to my eyes to see her better, but I still couldn't see her tits. That's when I noticed my hands had changed. They were small and dirty, and when I looked up, I wasn't in Kansas any more, Dorothy. I was standing in the picnic area down by the river in Wanaque. It only lasted for a few seconds, but for those seconds I was there. I could hear kids swimming at the beach, smell the hot dogs from someone's grill, could feel the stones from the ground digging into my knees as I knelt admiring the bottle cap. Even the mosquito sucking blood out of my arm before I swatted it with my other hand seemed real. Then, as suddenly as it had appeared, the vision was gone. Well, not exactly gone. I still had the bottle cap and there was a dead mosquito and a smear of blood on my right forearm.

If that had been the only incident like that I would have chalked it up to weird and forgotten about it. But when I pulled a 1954 Tops baseball card out of my back pocket with Yogi Berra's picture on it, I knew things had gone way past weird. The card was new and as soon as I saw what it was, I was back in Wanaque again, this time flipping cards with my best friend Goose Gaffney. We were playing "touchies" for keeps. I had already scored two touches and if I got one more I would win all the cards lying on the ground in front of us. Without even thinking, a flick of my wrist sent lucky Yogi spinning into the air in front of me. It curved right, ascended and then descended in a graceful arc and fell face down on another card. Touchie, I win!

Then, just as suddenly as I had been transported to Wanaque, I was back in my own home, in my own body, staring at a Tops baseball card lying on the living room carpet wondering what the hell had just happened. I was almost afraid to touch the familiar green back of the card, so I poked it once or twice with my index finger to see what would happen. When it didn't burst into flame, or send shocks up my arm, I picked it up and turned it over. Sure enough, there was Yogi, looking as cornpone as ever.

Later, I sat with the card in one hand and a cold Bud in the other thinking about flipping cards with Goose – my best friend and my fiercest rival. Everything we did was a competition. If he jumped off a cliff into the river, I had to jump off a higher cliff. If I got a new bike, he needed a newer bike. Our games of Mumbly Peg were especially nasty – the winner got to stick the peg anywhere he wanted, as long as there was a half-inch of peg showing, and the loser had to pull it out with his teeth. We had to stop playing after Goose made me pull a peg out of a pile of fresh dog shit and I retaliated by making him pull one out of a ground-hornet's nest.

Goose's real name was William but everyone all called him Goose because he honked when he got to laughing really hard. It was like honk, honk, honk . . . and then he'd realize what he was doing and honk even louder. Goose was my best friend back then, had been since the day he moved in next door when we were both five. Man, I hadn't thought of him in years. He moved away when we were ten and I never saw him again. Never even got a letter or a post card. I wonder where he is now and if he ever thinks about me?

The next thing I found in my jeans pocket was a steel ball about the size of a pea. It was tarnished and pitted with rust. As soon as I saw it I could see myself slipping it into the leather saddle of my first Wham-O slingshot. Goose and I both had one and we used them to decimate the frog population along the banks of the river. It really was a river back then, before the damn in Pompton Lakes broke and turned it into a pathetic trickle. Now I was taking careful aim on a squirrel that was clinging head down on a fat oak tree. I extended my left arm, drew my right hand back to my cheek and let fly. I could see the steel shot as it rocketed toward the unsuspecting tree rat. I even heard the "WHACK" when it slammed into the oak three inches below the squirrel's head.

Then, just as suddenly as I had been transported back in time, I was in my own body staring at my now empty hand. No steel ball, no slingshot, nothing – just an empty hand with slightly arthritic fingers.

Next out was a Boy Scout penknife – the kind with two blades, a can opener, and a bottle opener. I was kneeling in front of a campfire, holding the knife to my wrist. Goose was staring at me over the flames, waiting for me to draw the blade across my arm. He had already cut his and was impatiently waiting for me to cut mine.

"Come on, do it," he said. "Or don't you want to be my blood brother?"

When I still hesitated, he said, "What's the matter, chicken?"

That did it. I closed my eyes and quickly drew the blade across my wrist. When I looked down I was bleeding like a stuck pig.

The sounds of horns blaring brought me out of the vision. I dropped the knife on the seat beside me and drove to the tollbooth (God I hate those tollbooths), where I handed the attendant a five. As I held my arm out the window waiting for my change, I watched the sleeve of my dress shirt turn red. I quickly turned my hand over so the attendant wouldn't notice it. When I finally got my change I sped out of the tollbooth like I was afraid the car behind me might suddenly reach out and bite mine.

When I was safely back on the road I tore my blood-stained sleeve open to see how badly I was cut. To my surprise, except for the thin white line of the old scar, my wrist was unmarked. That freaked me out. Up until then, I could blow this stuff off. The mosquito could have been a coincidence. The stuff in my pockets, I could have bought it and forgotten about it (not likely but I could have), but the blood on my shirt, that I couldn't explain no matter how I tried. It was still wet and I had watched the sleeve turn red for Christ's sake.

I couldn't help wonder if Goose, wherever he was, was sharing this experience with me. Was he the yin to my yang? Every time I had been spirited off to the past he has been there, never anyone else, just Goose. I mean Goose was my best friend, but he wasn't my only friend – but for some reason, he was always the one who showed up in my visions. Whatever was happening was weird and I knew that he was tied into it somehow.

The day I found a .22 long-rifle cartridge rattling around in the bottom of my clothes dryer I was totally confused until I reached in and picked it up. Then I remembered when I had finally outdone Goose and there was nothing he could do about it. My Dad was into guns and Goose's wasn't. What was worse, his Mom was absolutely paranoid about the things. She wouldn't even let his Dad have one in the house. Hell, I had to loan him my old BB gun when we went out shooting in the woods. Well, for my birthday, my Dad got me a Savage .22/410 over/under combination rifle/shotgun. It took a .22 cartridge in the upper chamber and a 410-gauge shotgun shell in the lower one. Goose was green with envy and I knew it. And he knew I knew it, and that made it twice as sweet.

Goose almost shit when I showed him the over/under. "Have you got any shells for it?" he asked eagerly, and with more than a little touch of awe in his voice. I didn't say a word, I just reached into my pocket and pulled out a box of .22 Remington long-rifles.

"Damn," he said, his voice an excited whisper. "When can we take it out?"

The answer should have been, "Not till my Dad gets home," but I was too full of myself, and Goose's envy, to admit that. Instead, I said, "Let's do it now, but we'll have to sneak it out past my Mom."

"OK!" Goose agreed and nearly ran out of my room in his hurry to get outside. "Bye Mrs. Scott," I heard him call as the screen door slammed shut.

In less than a minute, he was standing outside my bedroom window waiting for me to hand him the gun. I passed it out, closed the window, and followed him out of the house. When I got outside Goose was nowhere to be seen, but I had expected that. He was already in the woods with the gun. He'd be waiting for me at the "foundation," the stone remains of an old Dupont building that had been abandoned long before we were born. We spent the rest of the day plinking at cans, bottles, and any creature unlucky enough to cross our path.

Tonight when I took my hand out of my pocket it contained forty-nine cents – one liberty head quarter, a Morgan dime, a buffalo nickel, a Jefferson nickel, and four wheat pennies. Forty-nine cents. God, the memories those few coins dragged out my subconscious. Memories I had suppressed for forty-nine years. Somehow, Goose's Dad had talked his mother into letting him have a shotgun for his birthday. He bought him a 12-guage! A 12-guage for Christ's sake, and all I had was a lousy 410. This time I was the one who was envious and Goose knew it. The .22 was good for plinking and stuff, but for hunting the 410 was no match for the 12-guage.

Since we were both fourteen, and had our licenses, we spent most of our time in the woods hunting. Goose spent most of that time asking me what I was going to do when deer season came. He loved telling me I couldn't use the .22, and even if I could get slugs for the 410 it wasn't big enough to bring down a deer. He kept laughing and telling me he'd bring it down for me if I could slow one down with the .410.

Seeing Goose's laughing face brought everything else that had happened that day back in a rush. Once again I was peering down the barrel of the Savage waiting for a good shot at a squirrel I had seen. I was lying on the ground, resting the barrel on a fallen tree trunk to steady my aim. I had a magnum cartridge in the chamber to give the .22 a little extra kick. When Goose stepped out from behind tree that had been obscuring him from my vantage point, I hardly hesitated, I just shot him in the chest. I didn't know why I did it then, and I still don't now. But that doesn't change anything, I still shot my best friend.

For a minute or two nothing happed, Goose just stared down at his chest like he was looking for something. Then he sort of melted to the ground, like his bones had turned to Jell-O. That's when I knew I had hit him, and the enormity of what I had done hit me.

"Goose. Jesus Christ, Goose, don't die!" I yelled as I ran across the twenty yards of ground that separated us.

"You shot me," he mumbled in disbelief when I reached him.

"It was an accident!" I lied. "The gun just went off."

"Am I going to die?" he asked me calmly. There was no fear in his voice but I think he was in shock by then.

"No," I told him. "You're going to be fine."

Goose coughed then and a trickle of blood seeped between his lips. Then he coughed a second time, harder, and he must have pulled the trigger of the 12-guage because the damn thing went off and blew a chunk out of my thigh.

Shit, I thought as I watched the blood pour out of the hole in my leg. *We're both gonna fuckin' die.*

I think I was on the verge of passing out when I heard a deep, sonorous chuckle and then someone said, "My, my, what have you two boys done to yourselves?"

I looked up and saw a tall, thin man silhouetted against an impossibly blue October sky. His suit, shirt, shoes, and tie were black. His overly bushy eyebrows looked like they might have been carved from coal. His skin was dark with oddly reddish undertones.

"You know you're going to die, don't you?" he said, as he sat down on a tree stump so his face would be closer to ours.

I started to answer but got distracted from the wisps of smoke rising up from the stump he was sitting on. The smell of burning wood and something else tainted the air. The smoke entwined about his head like a wavering nimbus. It made him look like a God, but I knew who he was – Satan, Prince of Lies, patron saint of all fourteen year-old boys who kill their best friends.

"What do you want?" I asked, knowing what his answer would be. My soul was what he wanted.

But he surprised me by saying, "Why, to help you of course."

"You . . . you mean you don't want my soul?" I stammered.

"That's already mine. Or it will be as soon as he dies," he answered, nodding at Goose who was still sitting up staring glassy-eyed at us.

"Then why would you want to help me?" I asked suspiciously.

"Curiosity, a whim, a diversion, call it what you will. I just want to see what you'll do with your life if I give you a few extra years. I find damned souls can be quite amusing."

"How many years?"

"Does it matter? Even one year would be more than you've got in front of you now. But, I'll tell you what. I'm a sporting man. Why don't we say one year for each cent you have in your pockets."

How much money did I have on me? I wasn't sure, and when I started to reach into my pocket he stopped me, saying, "No checking first. If I'm willing to take a chance here, you have to take one to. Choose now, before you look."

"What about Goose?" I asked, glancing at my friend. I was dismayed to see he had toppled onto his side and was staring blankly into space, his breathing erratic and shallow.

"He's not part of the equation." He answered. Then he said. "Choose now, or the deals off."

"OK, I'll do it," I blurted out.

"Done," he said, and smiled as he touched my forehead with his index finger. I felt an immediate stab of pain and I heard the skin sizzle. Then he turned and walked away, not even waiting for me to check my pockets to see how many years I had bought for myself. When he had disappeared into the trees I dug through every pocket I had and came up with exactly forty-nine cents: one quarter, one dime, two nickels, and four pennies.

I don't know how long I sat staring at those coins, but eventually another hunter found us. By that time Goose was dead and, surprisingly, my leg had stopped bleeding. Turns out the wound wasn't all that bad – it bled like hell but it was never life threatening. I'd like to think it had stopped before my pact with the devil, but I'm not sure. Maybe he suckered me into that deal. Anyway, it was over and done with and so are my forty-nine years. Now I'm sitting here waiting for him to come and collect his due.

Shit, I don't know how I blocked all these memories out of my mind for so long, but I did. And now they're back, retrieved by the same coins I remember dropping into Goose's casket before they closed the lid for the last time.

Christ, what have I gotten myself into? I sold my soul for forty-nine years and they weren't even good ones. Two marriages, two divorces, no kids, no friends unless you count Mr. Jim Beam and now I'm going to Hell, literally. Why couldn't I have turned him down? Why couldn't Goose's shot have been two feet higher? Why everything?

When I heard the knock on the door I didn't want to answer it, but I had to, had no choice really. I knew who it was, and one way or another he would make his way into the house. There was no way I could stop him or hide from him. The second knock came just before I placed my hand on the knob – this one was louder and sounded impatient. The calm I had wrapped myself in evaporated as I nervously turned the handle and opened the door.

"Hey Buddy, how you doing?" Goose greeted me from across the sill. "So, you gonna invite me in, or what?" I was too shocked to answer so I just stepped back and held the door open for him.

"Thanks," he said, smiling as he walked past me into the house. "I knew I could count on you. Yep, I could always count on my old buddy Wren (he was the only one who ever called me that)." I closed the door and followed him as he led me through the house to the den. From what I could see when I opened the door, and from following him now, he hadn't changed a bit since the day I had killed him – he was still wearing the same old blue jeans, Converse sneakers, Brooklyn Dodgers ball cap, (I was always a Yankee's fan) Levi's jacket, and under it, a bloodstained chambray shirt.

"So how's it hanging, old buddy? Bet you didn't expect to see me tonight, did you?"

"Where's . . .?" I stammered.

"Oh, he'll be along later. I just wanted to say hi and thank you for all you did for me before he got here."

"What do you mean, "all I did for you?", I killed you."

"Naw," he laughed, "Never happened. Well, you sure as hell shot me, that's for sure." Then he started laughing again.

"What's so funny?" I asked, bewildered.

"Sure as Hell, get it? Sure as Hell? Well, never mind, at least I think it's funny. Sure as Hell, ha! You still don't get it do you? Well let me spell it out for you. It's like this," he said, and then snapped his fingers. Sparks flew and a flame erupted from his index finger like it was a candle. Then he pointed it as me like it was a pistol and made little shooting motions. Each time he did, the flame jumped out at me like it was coming from a blowtorch. "I was never your friend, your good buddy Goose, I was just a damned soul doing my job, suckering in another fool for the Boss."

His words shocked and sickened me. It was the final betrayal. Even though I know I killed him, the only really good memories I have all involve Goose. And now I know they were all a charade. He was acting out a part to help damn me. My realization of this must have shown on my face because he laughed at me again and said, "Now you're getting it."

"Why did you do it?" I asked.

"Why? Because it's my job –it's what I do. Besides, it's either that, or burn in the fires of Hell. Personally, I prefer this."

"But you're helping to damn people. You helped damn me."

"No I didn't, you damned yourself. All I did was give you the opportunity. You could have turned the Boss down, but you didn't. You could have told him no and sent him packing. But you were too weak and you sold your soul for a lousy forty-nine more years of life. But shit, you didn't know that when you made the deal. What if you'd only had a penny. Pretty cheap for an eternity in Hell, don't you think?"

Listening to him, I was starting to remember why I had shot him in the first place. Even though I now knew whom, or rather what, he was, I still felt the need to compete with him, to be better than him. That's why the next thing I said was, "Well, I may be damned, but I won't be trying to trap others into selling their souls. At least I'll have that bit of integrity to take with me."

"Big deal," he answered but I could tell I'd scored with that one. Before I could press it another knock sounded from the front door.

"That's the Boss, best not to keep him waiting," Goose announced as he scrambled out of the chair he had commandeered. He left the room at a run and was back in less than a minute, following on the heels of the man who had approached me that fateful day in the woods.

"Well, Brandon, it's time. I hope your forty-nine years were well spent." When I didn't answer he said, "I'll take your silence as a no. Well, that's too bad. I guess it wasn't what you thought it would be," he said with a smile. "Almost time," he said, looking at his watch.

"Remember what I said," I told Goose. Before he could answer, the room was gone and my body was engulfed in pain. It seared every part of me. I could actually feel my skin, my internal organs, my brain, even my hair, and they were all in agony. But as bad as the pain was, the utter despair that filled me was even worse, knowing I had an eternity of this endure. It didn't take more than a second for me to decide I would damn my own mother if it would get me out of here. Then, just as suddenly as it had started, it was over and I was back in my family room facing Satan and Goose.

"So Brandon, how did you like your little glimpse of your future?"

I was still in shock from the instant I had spent in Hell. I had always joked that living in Jersey was Hell but now I knew what Hell really was. I'd take Jersey any day. Anyway, I knew enough to answer him when he addressed a question at me and I was struggling to get the words out of my mouth when he said, "No need to answer, I know how you feel. You can listen while I talk.

"My assistant," he said, nodding at Goose, "has intervened on your behalf. He tells me he thinks you would make an excellent recruiter. Now normally, I wouldn't do this, but I value his opinion so I'm willing to give you a try. You'll report directly to him of course, and if you don't measure up you'll have to return to Hell."

I tried to answer him but my throat was still raw from the pain I had experienced so I just nodded instead.

"Well, now that that's settled I'll leave you in the care of Mr. Gallows."

"Thanks Goose," I managed to choke out when I could finally talk.

"That's Sir, or Mr. Gallows, to you," he said, with a condescending sneer. "And it will be for as long as you expect to stay in this position."

"Yes Sir," I managed to choke out. All thoughts of showing him up lost in my fear of the power he now held over me.

What inspired "Forty-Nine Cents"?

Parts of this story are real. I did have a best friend (his name was Gip, not Honk) who moved away. We were in 5th grade at the time. We did collect bottle caps, flip baseball cards and compete at everything. The Mumbly Peg games really happened, even the dog shit part. So the loss part of this story was real. I did have a Savage 22/410 and used it to hunt most of the critters in the woods around Wanaque but Gip was log gone by then. Old Scratch showed up because everyone has to write a meet the Devil story sooner or later. This was mine.

Doc Johnson
F. Paul Wilson

F. Paul Wilson is the award-winning, bestselling author of thirty-five novels and nearly one hundred short stories. His novels The Keep, The Tomb, *and* Harbingers *appeared on the New York Times Bestsellers List.* The Tomb *received the 1984 Porgie Award from The West Coast Review of Books;* Wheels Within Wheels *won the first Prometheus Award. His novella "Aftershock" won a Stoker Award. He is listed in the 50th anniversary edition of* Who's Who in America. *Over eight million copies of his books are in print in the US and his work has been translated into twenty-four languages. He also has written for the stage, screen, and interactive media. Many of his recent novels have featured his popular antihero, Repairman Jack. His most recent novels are* Harbingers *and* Bloodline.

Currently he resides at the Jersey Shore where he is working on a young adult Repairman Jack novel and haunting eBay for weird clocks and Daddy Warbucks memorabilia. (He can also be found on the Web at www.repairmanjack.com*)*

Dark Territories   *F. Paul Wilson*

"*I* think you'd better take the call on oh-one," Jessie said, poking her head into the consultation room.

I glanced up from the latest issue of *Cardiology* and looked at my wife. It was Monday morning and I had a grand total of three patients scheduled.

"Why?"

"Because I said so."

That's what I get for hiring my wife as my nurse-receptionist, but I had to keep overhead down until I built up a decent practice and could afford a stranger . . . someone I could reprimand without paying for it later at home. I had to admit, though, Jessie was doing a damn fine job so far. She wasn't letting the pregnancy slow her down a bit.

"Who is it?"

She shrugged. "Not sure. Says she's never been here before but says her husband needs a doctor real bad."

"Got it."

Never turn down a patient in need. Especially one who might be able to pay. I picked up the phone.

"Hello. Doctor Reid."

"Oh, Doctor," said a woman's voice. "My husband's awful sick. Can you come see him?"

"A *house call?*" After all, I was a board-eligible internist. House calls were for GPs and family practitioners, not specialists. "What's wrong with your husband, Mrs. . . .?"

"Mosely—Martha Mosely. My husband, Joseph, he's . . . he's just not right. Sometimes he says he wants a doctor and sometimes he says he doesn't. He says he wants one now."

"Can you be a little more specific?"

If this Mosely fellow was going to end up in the hospital, I'd rather have him transported there first and then see him.

"I wish I could, Doctor, but I can't."

"Who's his regular doctor?"

"Doc Johnson."

Ah-ha!

"And why aren't you calling him?"

"Joe won't let me. He says he doesn't ever want to see Doc Johnson again. He only wants you."

I hesitated. I didn't want to get into the house-call habit, but as the new kid in town, I couldn't afford to pass up a chance to score some points.

"All right. Give me the address and I'll be out after dinner."

*

He doesn't ever want to see Doc Johnson again.

I thought about that as I drove out to the Mosely house. An odd thing to say. Most people in Ludlum Bay swore by Johnson. You'd think he walked on water the way some of them talked. Which wasn't making it any easier for me to get started in the Bay. I'd been living—quite literally—off the crumbs he left behind. Joseph Mosely appeared to be a crumb, so I was on my way to gather him up.

I turned south off Port Boulevard onto New Hope Road, watching the homes change from post-World War II tract homes to smaller, older houses on bigger lots. The January wind slapped at my car.

This was my first winter in Ludlum Bay and it was *cold.* I grew up in Florida, went to med school and did my internal medicine residency at Emory in Atlanta. My idea of cold and these New Jerseyans' idea of cold differed by a good twenty degrees.

The Bay natives like to say the nearness of the Atlantic tends to moderate the severity of the weather. Maybe that's true. According to the thermometer, it doesn't seem to get quite as cold here as it does inland, but I think the extra moisture sends the chill straight through to the bone.

But now the cold was locked outside the car and I was warm within. I had a bellyful of Jessie's tuna casserole, the Civic's heater-defrost system was blowing hard and warm. Snow blanketed the lawns and was banked on the curbs, but the asphalt was clean and dry. A beautiful, crystalline winter night for a drive. Too bad Jessie wasn't along. Too bad this wasn't a pleasure drive. People attach such rosy nostalgia to the house call, but here in the twenty-first century the house is a *lousy* place to practice medicine.

I slowed as the numbers on the mailboxes told me I was nearing the Mosely place. There: 620 New Hope Road. As I pulled into the driveway my headlamps lit up the house and grounds. I stopped the car halfway through the turn and groaned.

The Mosely house was a mess.

Every neighborhood has one. You know the type of house I mean. You drive along a street lined with immaculately kept homes, all with freshly painted siding and manicured lawns, all picture-perfect . . . except for one. There's always one house with a front yard where even the weeds won't grow; the Christmas lights are still attached to the eaves even though it might be June; if the neighborhood is lucky, only one rusting auto will grace the front yard, and the house's previous coat of paint will have merely peeled away, exposing much of the original color of the siding. If the neighborhood is especially cursed, the front yard will sport two or more automobile hulks in various stages of refurbishment, and the occupant will have started to paint the derelict home a hot pink or a particularly noxious shade of green and then quit halfway through.

The Mosely house was New Hope Road's derelict.

I turned off my engine and, black bag in hand, stepped out into the cold. No path had been dug through the snow anywhere I could see, but I found a narrow path where it had been packed down by other feet before me. It led across the front lawn. At least I think it was a lawn. The glow from a nearby streetlight limned odd bumps and rises all over the front yard. I could only guess at what lay beneath. A blanket of snow hides a multitude of sins.

I got a closer look at the house as I carefully picked my way toward it. The front porch was an open affair with its overhang tilted at a crazy angle. The paint was particularly worn and dirty up to a level of about two feet. Looked like a dog had spent a lot of time there but I saw no paw prints and heard no barking. The light from within barely filtered through the window shades.

The front door opened before I could knock. A thin, fiftyish woman wearing an old blue housedress and a stretched-out brown cardigan stood there with her hand on the knob.

"I'm terribly sorry, Doctor," she said in a mousy voice, "but Joe's decided he don't want to see a doctor tonight."

"What?" My voice went hoarse with shock. "You mean to tell me I came—"

"Oh, let him in, Martha!" said a rough voice from somewhere behind her. "Long as he's here, might as well get a look at him."

"Yes, Joe."

She stepped aside and I stepped in.

The air within was hot, dry, and sour. I wondered how many years since they'd had the windows open. A wood stove sat in a corner to my left. The only light in the room came from candles and kerosene lamps.

Joseph Mosely, the same age as his wife but thinner, sat in a rocker facing me. His skin was stretched tight across his high forehead and cheekbones. He had a full head lank hair and a three-day stubble.

Something familiar about him. As I watched, he sipped from a four-ounce tumbler clutched in his right hand; a half-empty bottle of no-name gin sat on a small table next to him. He stared at me. I've seen prosthetic eyes of porcelain and glass show more warmth and human feeling than Joe Mosely's.

"If that was your idea of a joke, Mr. Mosely—"

"Don't bother trying to intimidate me, Doctor Charles Reid. It's a waste of breath. Take the man's coat, Martha."

"Yes, Joe."

Sighing resignedly, I shrugged out of my jacket and turned to hand it to her. I stopped and stared at her face. A large black-and-purple hematoma, a good inch and a half across, bloomed on her right cheek. I hadn't noticed it when she opened the door. But now . . . I knew from the look of it that it couldn't be more than a couple of hours old.

"Better get the ice back on that bruise," he said to her from his rocker. "And careful you don't slip on the kitchen floor and hurt yourself again."

"Yes, Joe."

Clenching my teeth against the challenge that leaped into my throat, I handed her my coat and turned to her husband.

"What seems to be the problem, Mr. Mosely?"

He put the glass down and rolled up his right sleeve to show me a healing laceration on the underside of his forearm.

"This."

It ran up from the wrist for about five inches or so and looked to be about ten days to two weeks old. Three silk sutures were still in place.

My anger flared. "You brought me all the way out here for a suture removal?"

"*I* didn't bring you anywhere. You brought yourself. And besides—" He kicked up his left foot; it looked deformed within a dirty sock. "I'm disabled."

"All right," I said, cooling with effort. "How'd you cut yourself?"

"Whittling."

I felt like asking him if he'd been using a machete, but restrained myself.

"They sew it up at County General?"

"Nope."

"Then who?"

He paused and I saw that his eyes were even colder and flatter than before.

"Doc Johnson."

"Why'd he leave these three sutures in?"

"Didn't. Took them out myself. He won't ever get near me again—*ever!*" He half rose from the rocker. "I wouldn't take my *dog* to him if she was still alive!"

"Hey! Take it easy."

He calmed himself with another sip of gin.

"So why did *you* leave the last three in?"

He looked at the wound, then away.

" 'Cause there's something wrong with it."

I inspected it more closely. It looked fine. The wound edges had knitted nicely. Doc Johnson had done a good closure. I found no redness or swelling to indicate infection.

"Looks okay to me."

I opened my bag, got out an alcohol swab, and dabbed the wound. Then I took out scissors and forceps and removed those last three sutures.

"There. Good as new."

"There's *still* something wrong with it." He pulled his arm away to reach for the gin glass; he drained it, then slammed it down. "There's something in there."

I almost laughed. "Pardon me?"

"Something's *in* there! I can feel it move every now and then. The first time was when I started taking the sutures out. There! Look!" He stiffened and pointed to the scar. "It's moving now!"

I looked and saw nothing the least bit out of the ordinary. But I thought I knew what was bothering him.

"Here." I took his left hand and laid the fingers over the underside of his forearm. "Press them here. Now, open and close your hand, making a fist. There . . . feel the tendons moving under the skin? You've probably got a little scar tissue building up in the deeper layers next to a tendon sheath and it's—"

"Something's *in* there, damn it! Doc Johnson put it there when he sewed me up!"

I stood. "That's ridiculous."

"It's true! I wouldn't make up something like that!"

"Did you watch him sew you up?"

"Yeah."

"Did you see him put anything in the wound?"

"No. But he's sneaky. I know he put something in there!"

"You'd better lay off the gin." I closed my bag. "You're having delusions."

"Shoulda known," he said bitterly, reaching for his bottle. "You doctors think you've got all the answers."

I took my coat off a hook by the door and pulled it on.

"What's that supposed to mean? And haven't you had enough of that for one night?"

"*Damn* you!" Eyes ablaze with fury, he hurled the glass across the room and leaped out of the rocker. "Who the hell do you think you are to tell me when I've had enough!"

He limped toward me and then I remembered why he looked familiar. The limp triggered it: I had seen him dozens of times in the Port Boulevard shopping area, usually entering or leaving Elmo's liquors. He'd lied to me—he wasn't disabled enough to warrant a house call.

"You're drunk." I reached for the doorknob. "Sleep it off."

Suddenly he stopped his advance and grinned maliciously.

"Oh, I'll sleep, all right. But will *you?* Better pray nothing goes bad with this arm here, or you'll have another malpractice case on your hands. Like the one in Atlanta."

My stomach wrenched into a tight ball. "How do you know about that?"

I hoped I didn't look as sick as I felt.

"Checked into you. When I heard we had this brand-new doctor in town, fresh from a big medical center in Atlanta, I asked myself why a young, hot-shot specialist would want to practice in the Bay? So I did some digging. I'm real good at digging. 'Specially on doctors. They got these high an' mighty ways with how they dole out pills and advice like they're better'n the rest of us. Doctor Tanner was like that. That office you're in used to be his. I dug up some *good* dirt on Tanner but he disappeared before I could rub his face in it."

"Good night."

I stepped out on the porch and pulled the door closed behind me.

I had nothing else to say. I thought I'd left that malpractice nightmare behind me in Atlanta. The realization that it had followed me here threatened all the hopes I'd nursed of finding peace in Ludlum Bay. And to hear it from the grinning lips of someone like Joe Mosely made me almost physically ill.

*

I barely remembered the trip home. I seemed to be driving through the past, through interrogatories and depositions and sweating testimonies. I didn't really come back to the present until I parked the car and walked toward the duplex we were renting.

Jessie was standing on the front steps, wrapped in her parka, arms folded across her chest as she looked up at the stars under a full moon. Suddenly I felt calm. This was the way I had found her when we first met— standing on a rooftop gazing up at the night sky, looking for Jupiter. She owned two telescopes she used regularly, but she's told me countless times that a true amateur astronomer never tires of naked-eye stargazing.

She smiled as she saw me walk up. "How was the house call?"

I put on an annoyed expression. "Unnecessary." I wouldn't tell her about tonight. At least one of us should rest easy. I patted her growing belly. "How we doing in there?"

"You mean the Tap Dance Kid? Active as ever."

She turned back to the stars and frowned. I followed her upward gaze.

"What's the matter?"

"I don't know. Something weird about the stars out here."

They looked all right to me, except that I could see a hell of a lot more of them than I'd ever seen in Atlanta.

Jessie slipped an arm around my back and seemed to read my expression without looking at me.

"Yeah. I said *weird.* They don't look right. I could get out a star map and I know everything would look fine. But something's just not right up there. The perspective's different somehow. Only another stargazer would notice. Something's wrong."

I had heard that expression too many times tonight.

"The baby wants to go in," I said. "He's cold."

"*She's* cold."

"Anything you say."

*

I had trouble sleeping that night. I kept reliving the malpractice case and how I wound up scapegoat for a couple of department heads at the medical center. After all, I was only a resident and they had national reputations. I was sure they were sleeping well tonight while I lay here awake.

I kept seeing the plaintiff attorney's hungry face, hearing his voice as he tore me apart. I'm a good doctor, a caring one who knows internal medicine inside and out, but you wouldn't have thought so after that lawyer was through with me. He got a third of the settlement and I got the word that I shouldn't apply for a position on the staff when my residency was up. I supposed the big shots didn't want me around as a reminder.

Jessie wanted me to fight them for an appointment but I knew better. Every hospital staff application has a question that reads: "Have you ever been denied staff privileges at any other hospital?" If you answer *Yes,* they want to know all the particulars. If you say *No,* and later they find out otherwise, your ass is grass.

Discretion is the better part of valor, I always say. I knew they'd turn me down, and I didn't want to answer *yes* to that question for the rest of my life. So I packed up and left when my residency was over. The medical center reciprocated by giving me good recommendations.

Jessie says I'm too scared of making waves. She's probably right. She usually is. I do know I couldn't have made it through the trial without her. She stuck by me all the way.

She's right about the waves, though. All I want to do is live in peace and quiet and practice the medicine I've been trained for. That's all. I don't need a Porsche or a mansion. Just Jessie and our kids and enough to live comfortably. That's all I want. That's all I've ever wanted.

*

Wednesday afternoon, two days after the Mosely house call, I was standing on Doc Johnson's front porch, ringing his bell.

"Stop by the house this afternoon," he'd said on the phone a few hours ago. "Let's get acquainted."

I'd been in town seven months now and this was the first time he'd spoken to me beyond a nod and a good-morning while passing in the hall at County General. I couldn't use the excuse that my office was too busy for me to get away, so I accepted. Besides, I was curious as to why he wanted to see me.

I'd spotted Joe Mosely on my way over. He was coming out of the liquor store and saw me waiting at the light. He looked terrible. I wasn't sure if it was just the daylight or if he was actually thinner than the other night. His cheeks looked more sunken, his eyes more feverish. But his smile hadn't changed. The way he grinned at me had tied my stomach into a knot that was just now beginning to unravel.

I tried not to think of Mosely as I waited for someone to answer my ring. I inspected my surroundings. The Johnson house was as solid as they come, with walls built of the heavy gray native granite that rimmed the shore in these parts. Little mortar was visible. Someone had taken great pains to mate each stone nook and cranny against its neighbor. The resultant pattern was like the flip side of one of those thousand-piece Springbok jigsaw puzzles that Jessie liked to fiddle with.

His verandah here high on East Hill—the only real hill in town—offered a clear eastward view of the length and breadth of the bay all the way down to Blind Point; beyond the barrier island the Atlantic surged cold and gray. To the west lay the Parkway—the low drone of its traffic was audible most nights, but that was a minor concern when you considered how easy it made getting to places like picturesque Cape May to the south and glitzy Atlantic City to the north.

And beyond the Parkway, the deep and enigmatic Jersey Pine Barrens.

I could get used to this.

I thought about Doc Johnson. I'd heard he was a widower with no children, that his family had come over with Ludlum Bay's original settlers back in the seventeenth century. Doctors apparently came and went pretty regularly around the Bay, but "the Doc"— that's what the natives called him—was as constant as the moon, always available, always willing to come out to the house should you be too sick to go to him. If you were a regular patient of the Doc's he never let you down. People talked as if he'd always been here and always would. His practice seemed to encompass the whole town. That was impossible, of course. No one man could care for 20,000 people. But to hear folks talk—and to listen to the grumbling of the few other struggling doctors in town—that was the way it was.

The handle rattled and Doc Johnson opened the door himself. A portly man in his sixties with a full, friendly, florid face and lots of white hair combed straight back, he wore a white shirt, open at the collar, white duck pants, and a blue blazer with a gold emblem on the breast pocket. He looked more like a yacht club commodore than a doctor.

"Charles!" he said, shaking my hand. "So good of you to come! Come in out of the chill and I'll make you a drink!"

It wasn't as chilly as it had been the past few days but I was glad to step into the warmth. He was fixing himself a Sapphire gimlet with a dash of Cointreau and offered me one. I was through for the day, so I accepted. It was excellent.

He showed me around the house that one of his ancestors had built a couple of centuries ago. We made small talk during the tour until we ended up in his study before a fire. He was a gracious, amiable host and I took an immediate liking to him.

"Let's talk shop a minute," he said after I refused a refill on the gimlet and we'd settled into chairs. "I like to feel out a new doctor in town on his philosophy of medicine." His eyes penetrated mine. "Do you have one?"

I thought about that. Since starting med school I'd been so involved in learning whatever there was to know about medicine that I hadn't given much consideration to a philosophical approach. I was tempted to say *Keeping my head above water* but thought better of it. I decided to go Hippocratic.

"I guess I'd start with 'Above all else do no harm.''

He smiled. "An excellent start. But how would triage fit into your philosophy, Horatio?"

"Horatio?"

"I'm an avid reader. You will forgive me a literary reference once in a while, won't you? That was to *Hamlet*. A strained reference, I'll grant you, but *Hamlet* nonetheless."

"Of course. But triage . . .?"

"Under certain circumstances we have to choose those who will get care and those who won't. In disasters, for instance: We must ignore those whom we judge to be beyond help in order to aid those who are salvageable."

"Of course. That's an accepted part of emergency care."

"But aren't you doing harm by withholding care?"

"Not if a patient is terminal. Not if the outcome will remain unchanged no matter what you do."

"Which means we must place great faith in our judgment, then, correct?"

I nodded. "Yes, I suppose so."

Where was this going?

"And what if one must amputate a gangrenous limb in order to preserve the health of the rest of the body? Isn't that doing harm of sorts to the diseased limb?"

I said, "I suppose you could look at it that way, but if the health of the good tissue is threatened by the infected limb, and you can't cure the infection, then the limb's got to go."

"Precisely. It's another form of triage: The diseased limb must be lopped off and discarded. Sometimes I find that triage must be of a more active sort where radical decisions must be made. Medicine is full of life-and-death decisions, don't you think?"

I nodded once more. What a baffling conversation.

"I understand you had the pleasure of meeting the estimable Joseph Mosely the other night."

The abrupt change of subject left me reeling for a second.

"I don't know if I'd call it a pleasure."

He barked a laugh. "There'd be something seriously wrong with you if you did. A despicable excuse for a human being. Truly a hollow man, if you'll excuse the Yeats reference—or is that Eliot? No matter. It fits Joe Mosely well enough: no heart, no soul. An alcoholic who abused his children mercilessly. I patched up enough cuts and contusions on his battered boys, and I fear he battered his only daughter in a far more loathsome way. They all ran away as soon as they were able. So now he abuses poor Martha when the mood suits him, and that is too often. Last summer I had to strap up three broken ribs on that poor woman. But she won't press charges. Love's funny, isn't it?"

"It is," I said. "But codependency isn't."

"You've got that right. Did you notice his mangled foot, by the way? That happened when he was working at the shoe factory. Talk is he stuck his foot in one of the machines on purpose, only he stuck it in farther than he intended and did too good a job of injuring himself. Anyway, he got a nice settlement out of it, which is what he wanted, but he drank it up in no time."

"I'm not surprised," I said, remembering his rapidly dwindling level in his gin bottle.

"And did you notice the lack of electricity? The power company caught him tampering with the meter and cut him off. I've heard he's blackmailing a few people in town. And he steals anything that's not nailed down. That cut on his arm I sewed up? That was the first time in all these years I'd ever had a chance to actually treat him. He tried to tell me he did it whittling. Ha! Never yet seen a right-handed man cut his right arm with a knife. No, he did that breaking into a house on Armondo Street. Did it on a storm window. Read in the *Gazette* how they found lots of blood at the scene and were checking ERs in the area to see if anybody had been sewn up. That was why he came to me. I tell you, he will make the world a brighter place by departing it."

"You didn't report him to the police?"

"No," he said levelly. "And I don't intend to. The courts won't give him his due. And calling the police is not my way of handling the likes of Joe Mosely."

I had to say it: "Mosely says you put something in the laceration when you sewed it up."

Doc Johnson's face darkened. "I hope you will consider the source and not repeat that."

"Of course not. I only mentioned it now because you were the accused."

"Good." He cleared his throat. "There's some things you should know about the Bay. We like it quiet here. We don't like idle chatter. You'll find that things have a way of working themselves out in their own way. You don't get outsiders involved if you can help it."

"Like me?"

"That's up to you, Charles. You can be an insider if you want to be. 'Newcomer' and 'insider' aren't mutually exclusive terms in Ludlum Bay. A town dies if it doesn't get *some* new blood. But discretion is all important. As a doctor in town you may occasionally see something out of the ordinary. You can take it as it comes, deal with it, and leave it at that—which will bring you closer to the inside. Or, you can talk about it a lot or maybe even submit a paper on it to something like the *New England Journal of Medicine,* and that will push you out. *Far* out. Soon you'd have to pack up and move away."

He stood and patted my shoulder.

"I like you, Charles. This town needs more doctors. I'd like to see you make it here."

"I'd like to stay here."

"Good! I do my own sort of triage on incoming doctors. If I think they'll work out, I send them my overflow." He sighed. "And believe me, I'm getting ready to increase my overflow. I'd like to slow down a bit. Not as young as I used to be."

"I'd appreciate that."

He gave me a calculating look. "Okay. We'll see. But first— " He glanced outside. "Well, here it comes!" He motioned me over to the big bay window. "Take a look!"

I stepped to his side and gazed out at the Atlantic—or rather, where the Atlantic had been. The horizon was gone, lost in a fog bank that was even now rolling into the bay itself.

Doc Johnson pointed south. "If you watch, you'll see Blind Pew disappear."

"Excuse me?"

He laughed. "Another reference, my boy. I've called Blind Point 'Blind Pew' ever since I read *Treasure Island* when I was ten. You remember Blind Pew, don't you?"

N. C. Wyeth's painting of the moonlit character suddenly flashed before my eyes. It had always given me the chills.

"Of course. But where's the fog coming from?"

"The Gulf Stream. For reasons known only to itself, it swings in here a couple of times a winter. The warm air from the stream hits the cold air on the land and then we have fog. And I do mean *fog*."

As I watched, lacy fingers of mist began to rise from the snow in the front yard.

"Yes, sir!" he said, rubbing his hands together and smiling. "This one's going to be a beauty!"

*

Mrs. Mosely called me Friday night.

"Doctor, you've got to come out and see Joe."

"No, thank you," I told her. "Once was quite enough."

"I think he's dying!"

"Then get him over to County General."

"He won't let me call an ambulance. He won't let me near him!"

"Then I'm sorry—"

"*Please*, Doctor Reid!" Her voice broke into a wail. "If not for him, then for me! I'm frightened!"

Something in her voice got to me. And I remembered that bruise on her cheek.

"Okay," I said reluctantly. "I'll be over in a half hour."

I knew I'd regret it.

*

The fog was still menacingly thick, and worse at night than during the day. At least you could pick out shadows in daylight. At night the headlights bounced off the fog instead of penetrating it. Like driving through cotton.

When I finally reached the Mosely place, the air seemed cooler and the fog appeared to be thinning. Somewhere above, moonlight struggled to get through. Maybe the predicted cold front from the west was finally moving in.

Martha Mosely opened the door.

"Thank you for coming, Doctor Reid. I don't know what to do! He won't let me touch him or go near him! I'm at my wit's end!"

"Where is he?"

"In bed."

She led me to a room in the back and stood at the door clutching her hands between her breasts as I entered.

By the light of the room's single flickering candle I could see Joe Mosely lying naked on the bed, stretched out like an emaciated corpse. In fact, for a moment I thought he was dead—his breathing was so shallow I couldn't see his chest move.

Then he turned his head a few degrees in my direction.

"So, it's you." His lips barely moved. The eyes were the only things alive in his face.

"Yeah. Me. What can I do for you?"

"First, you can close the door—with that woman on the other side."

Before I could answer, I heard the door close behind me. I was alone in the room with him.

"And second, you can keep your distance."

"What's the matter? Anything hurt?"

"No pain. But I'm a dead man. It's Doc Johnson's doing. I told you he put something in that cut."

His words were disturbing enough, but his completely emotionless tone made them even more chilling—as if whatever emotions he possessed had been drained away along with his vitality.

"You need to be hospitalized."

"No use. I'm already gone. But let me tell you about Doc Johnson. He did this to me. He's got his own ways and he follows his own rules. I've tailed him into the Pine Barrens a few times but I always lost him. Don't know what he goes there for, but it can't be for no good."

I took out my stethoscope as he raved. When he saw it, his voice rose in pitch.

"Don't come near me. Just keep away."

"Don't be ridiculous. I'm here. I might as well see if I can do anything for you."

I adjusted the earpieces and went down on one knee beside the bed.

"Don't! Keep back!"

I pressed the diaphragm over his heart to listen—

—and felt his chest wall give way like a stale soda cracker.

My left hand disappeared up to the wrist inside his chest cavity. And it was *cold* in there! I yanked it out and hurled myself away from the bed, not stopping until I came up against the bedroom wall.

"Now you've done it," he said in that passionless voice.

As I watched, a yellow mist began to ooze out of the opening. It slid over his ribs and along the sheet, and from there down to the floor, like the fog from dry ice.

I looked at Mosely's face and saw the light go out of his eyes.

He was gone.

A wind began blowing outside, whistling under the doors and banging the shutters. I glanced out the window on the far side of the room and saw the fog begin to swirl and tear apart. Suddenly something crashed in the front room. I pulled myself up and opened the bedroom door. A freezing wind hit me in the face with the force of a gale, tearing the door from my grip and swirling into the room. I saw Martha Mosely get up from the sofa and struggle to close the front door against the rage of the wind.

The bedroom window shattered under the sudden pressure and now the wind howled through the house.

The yellow mist from Mosely's chest cavity caught the gale and rode it out the window, slipping along the floor and up the wall and over the sill in streaks that gleamed in the growing moonlight.

Then the mist was gone and I was alone in the room with the wind and Joe Mosely's empty shell.

And then that shell began to crumble, caving in on itself piece by piece, almost in slow motion, fracturing into countless tiny pieces that in turn disintegrated into a gray, dust-like powder. This too was caught by the wind and carried out into the night.

Joe Mosely was gone, leaving behind not so much as a depression in the bedcovers.

The front door finally closed with Martha's efforts and I heard the bolt slide home. She walked up to the bedroom door but did not step inside.

"Joe's gone, isn't he?" she said in a low voice.

I couldn't speak. I opened my mouth but no words would come. I simply nodded as I stood there trembling.

She stepped into the room then and looked at the bed. She looked at the broken window, then at me.

With a sigh she sat on the edge of the bed and ran her hand over the spot where her husband had lain.

*

My home phone rang at eight o'clock the next morning. It didn't disturb my sleep. I'd been awake all night. Part of the time I'd spent lying rigid in bed, the rest here in the kitchen with all the lights on, waiting for the sun.

An awful wait. When I wasn't reliving the scene in the Mosely bedroom I was hearing voices. If it wasn't Joe telling me that Doc Johnson had put something in his wound, it was the Doc himself talking about making life-and-death decisions, about triage, all laced with literary references.

I hadn't told Jessie a thing. She'd think I was ready for a straitjacket. And if by some chance she *did* believe, she'd want to pack up and get out of town. But where to? We had the baby to think of.

I'd spent the time since dawn going over my options. And when the phone rang, I had no doubt who was calling.

"I understand Joe Mosely is gone," Doc Johnson said without preamble.

"Yes."

. . . a hollow man . . .

"Any idea where?"

"Out the window." My voice sounded half dead to me. "Beyond that, I don't know."

. . . calling the police is not my way of handling the likes of Joe Mosely . . .

"Seen anything lately worth writing to any of the medical journals about?"

"Not a thing."

. . . the diseased limb has to he lopped off and discarded . . .

"Just another day in Ludlum Bay then?" Doc Johnson said.

"Oh, I hope not." I could not hide the tremor in my voice.

. . . sometimes triage has to be of a more active sort where radical decisions must be made . . .

He chuckled. "Charles, my boy, I think you'll do all right here. As a matter of fact, I'd like to refer a couple of patients to your office today. They've got complicated problems that require more attention than I can give them at this time. I'll assure them that they can trust you implicitly. Will you take them on?"

I paused. Even though my mind was made up, I took a deep breath and held it, waiting for some argument to come out of the blue and swing me the other way. Finally, I could hold it no longer.

"Yes," I said. "Thank you."

"Charles, I think you're going to do just fine in Ludlum Bay."

What inspired "Doc Johnson"?

Primum non nocere. That's how the Hippocratic Oath begins: "First do no harm." A doctor often holds a patient's life in his hands. It's the ultimate power trip - if you're into that sort of thing. What if a doctor decided to perform a little triage? Physicians from time to time come into contact with patients whose passing would leave the world a brighter place. Their families and their community would be better of without them. Now, let's say you have a physician who has set himself up as a guardian of sorts, to protect his community from its predators and baser elements. Hmmm...

Hunger
Meghan Knierim

Meghan Knierim has had several short stories and poems published (under Meghan Fatras) in venues such as Horrorfind.com, Scared Naked Magazine, and the Garden State Horror Writers' anthologies In a Fearful State *and* Tales from a Darker State. *She was also an assistant editor for the now defunct Flesh and Blood Magazine and currently works as an editorial assistant at Cigar Magazine. She lives in NJ with her two children. You can learn more about Meghan by visiting her at:* http://morbidmusings.livejournal.com.

Natalia shifted in her seat as she pulled into the Broadway Diner's parking lot, her crotch still soaked after this evening's feeding. A pink, neon sign flashed "the best pancakes in Jersey." She hoped so. No matter how sick she felt inside when the hunger was appeased, genuine appetite always took its place. She would not sleep tonight, as usual, but the best pancakes in Jersey would help to settle her.

The diner bustled at two o'clock in the morning. An old lady sipped coffee at the far end of the counter, a young couple ate an early breakfast of eggs and bacon, a group of college boys horsed around and harassed the waitress at a booth in the back, and two old men at the table closest to the entrance barked at each other about the troop surge in Iraq. Natalia sat at the opposite end of the counter from the old woman. She had a good view of the rowdy young men.

She thumbed through the menu and overheard snippets of conversation between the hooligans and their waitress.

"Does the birthday boy want whipped cream?" The waitress danced around the booth. "Open up!" The kid did as he was instructed, and the waitress squirted Ready Whip straight into his mouth. His buddies hooted and hollered. Natalia couldn't help but smirk. *Ah, to be young.*

The waitress placed the container back into the pouch on her apron, and headed over to Natalia. "What'll you have?"

"Chocolate chip pancakes, please." She spied the Ready Whip nozzle sticking out of the woman's pouch and thought about how many dirty mouths it had been shoved into...then how many dirty cocks had been shoved into her. "No whip cream."

The waitress sighed as she took the menu and hurried into the kitchen. Natalia turned her head and caught the eye of one of the unruly boys. He was just a baby, no more than 21. His gaze held hers for a moment, he smiled. She smiled back.

Don't be stupid, ignore him. There was no need to pick up another one. The stranger from The Loop would last her a few days. She couldn't let herself be suckered by another pretty face — to destroy a life when she didn't need to would be immoral.

She turned back to her placemat and mulled over the night's events...how the stranger pounded into her from behind, grunted, and slapped her ass while she panted into his pillow and begged him to call her terrible names. She sighed and released a few unenthusiastic moans. She faked it well enough, but her heart wasn't in it, hadn't been in a long time.

She felt him tense up, this one of dark hair and light eyes, felt him cum inside her. He collapsed on the bed. The room became quiet but for his ragged breaths.

"So," he said, "it's getting late."

"And?"

"It's getting late, and you're still here."

"Fine, whatever you want."

Natalia didn't care he didn't want her hanging around. Hell, that's why she agreed to go home with him. She needed it. When that sensation came over her body, to not give in would kill her. She had her fill, and it was time to get the hell out of Dodge.

She threw on her clothes and grabbed her purse. As she walked out the door she thought he said something, but didn't bother to go back and find out. It didn't matter. He'd be dead soon anyway.

The longest any man ever lasted was three days —
her first, but that was a long time ago. They seemed to
kick off faster now. If she had just hung around a little
while longer, she might have seen it, but she flew out of
there, straight to her Acura, straight to the New Jersey
Turnpike, straight to the diner, straight to hell.

Tonight's escapade was random guy *216 who hit
on her at The Loop Lounge. He was attractive enough,
but at that point the cuteness factor meant nothing. Her
hunger was insatiable. If she had to, she would have
banged the old, toothless redneck who sat in the back.

Natalia considered her most recent nourishment.
Maybe this time it would be different. She tried not to
"go there," toward compassion. She would never know
what happened to him, and that was best. If she
allowed that, her guilt would eat her up, and she knew
better.

This is not your fault.

"Head's up, sugar." Her pancakes arrived. She
poured syrup over them, found herself glancing back to
the table of boys. They had quieted down. The cute
one looked up, caught her eye. They smiled at each
other, then she cast down her eyes. He reminded her of
Tim.

Tim was Natalia's first. She waited so long for him.
All of her friends had thrown away their innocence long
ago, but she wanted to believe in love before sacrificing
herself. It was her junior year in college, and she and
Tim had been together for almost a year. They were
snuggling on the couch in the common room, watching
Dawn of the Dead for the hundredth time.

Out of nowhere, he turned to her, looked deep into
her eyes, and said, "Do you know how much I love
you?"

Natalia blinked tears from her eyes as she remembered how she pulled him to her, kissed him, and whispered that she needed him, and she wanted to prove it.

She knew he wasn't a virgin, and she expected the first time would be painful and not enjoyable. He took care of her, though. He was gentle and sweet. He took his time, and made sure she was all right. It was beautiful, even if she didn't get off.

Three days later, he was gone. He went to the local 7-11 to buy a coffee. He didn't even see the gunman as he walked to the counter. Startled, the thief shot Tim, then the cashier.

Natalia didn't put it together with sex. She saw it as tragic bad timing. She didn't date again for almost two years, she couldn't bear it. But then Greg came along and everything changed. He swept her off her feet and, after dating for six months, she felt comfortable enough to give herself over to him. This time it was better for her, she climaxed. That was the beginning of the end...both for Greg, and for days before the hunger.

Greg was dead the next day. He slipped in the shower and slammed his head against the side of the tub. Natalia was beside herself. Still believing it was her shitty luck, she moved on, but it wasn't long before the hunger began.

It started one night as she prepared for bed. She felt a tingling sensation move up her thighs, she became flushed, her body began to sweat. Heat from her inner thighs traveled up inside her. Her clitoris stiffened as carnal thoughts overcame her. She had only ever had sex twice, but all she could think about was getting it. She began to panic.

Natalia tried rubbing her clit, so close to climax, but she couldn't. She was going crazy. The pains hit her then. Searing lava shooting through her veins, she cried out in ecstatic agony. *I have to get fucked!*

She threw on the closest pair of jeans and a t-shirt and ran out the door. Driving proved difficult as the pain knocked the wind out of her. She arrived at the Wild Irish Rose, the closest bar to her apartment. She didn't care who gave it to her, she just knew if she didn't get it soon, the pain would either drive her insane or kill her.

The bar patrons gawped at her as she stumbled into the pub. She looked a wreck, but knew one of these drunks would go for an easy hump. Natalia caught the eye of an older guy alone at a table in the corner. Salt and pepper stubble covered his strong chin, fine lines etched around his gray eyes. His forehead had deep furrows that peeked out from underneath a mop of messy, gray hair.

She walked over to him, tried to ignore the pain between her legs.

"Can I buy you a drink, little lady?" His speech was slow, he was more than half in the bag.

She leaned and whispered, "Let's skip the drinks. You got a car?"

Surprised, the man replied, "I've got a truck out back. You need a lift?"

"Take me to your truck, you'll get a lift." Natalia slid her hand into his lap. He became stiff through the denim bunched in his crotch.

He jumped up from the chair and grabbed her hand, rushed her to the exit — her hands were at his zipper as they climbed into the truck.

"Whoa, baby...you don't believe in foreplay?"

"Shut up and do me." She spit the words into his face as she fumbled his zipper. His sweat smelled like chewing tobacco.

The man pulled his jeans off as Natalia ripped hers from her body. He snapped the string of her thong and pushed her down onto the seat. He penetrated her and Natalia moaned. The pains were replaced by intense waves of pleasure. His hips pounded against her as her body filled with a bliss she never anticipated. She cried out, and he pressed deeper.

Her body shuddered and her legs locked up when she came. The man from the bar perspired as he pulled out of her. His face was drained of personality. He looked at her, and his breaths started to come at a quicker pace. He leaned against the door grasping his chest. Natalia was so softened by post-coital bliss that she didn't notice his distress until he started to groan. When she turned toward him, he was clawing at his chest, and then he was still.

The connection hit her then. She called the ambulance, but the man, George Flynn from Wharton, was pronounced dead at the scene. A heart attack, they said. The EMT told Natalia there was nothing she could have done. She knew, though, she killed him.

A clank of dishes brought Natalia back to reality. She stared at the confectionary mess in front of her. *How can I eat at a time like this?* Maybe she was just getting used to it. She'd rationalized her behavior for years. The one time she tried to deny her impulse was torture. She had no idea if it would have killed her, but the pain and madness were enough to keep her from finding out. This was survival, that was it. After George, the hunger kept coming back.

There didn't seem to be a set pattern, but the feeling came upon her at least once a month. She learned it didn't matter where she was or what she was doing — the moment she sensed it, she needed to find someone. Toys didn't work, neither did any form of masturbation

— it had to be flesh — stiff, male flesh. She once tried with another woman, but the pain became so bad she ran out in the middle and ended up plucking the neighborhood thug out of his yard. Smug little prick harassed all the young girls...so she gave him what he wanted — turned the bastard into a man. Within sixteen hours, his body was found in pieces across the railroad tracks.

After that episode she went to her doctor, who, of course, didn't believe her. After giving Natalia a thorough exam and not finding anything out of the ordinary, he referred her to a shrink.

Dr. Simmons tried to convince her that it was all in her head, that she'd had a string of bad luck and it was all coincidence. He told her the "hunger" was most likely a manifestation of past childhood trauma that she just wasn't remembering.

She knew the doc was a quack when his "therapy" sessions turned into nothing more than him getting off on her recounting the numerous feedings she'd experienced. After telling him she needed to leave her appointment one day because the hunger was creeping through her, Dr. Simmons said it would be good for her if she had sex with him, so he could prove she wasn't killing anyone.

Sick bastard had it coming. So she let him bend her over his black leather couch. He wasn't able to make the rest of his appointments that day, as he had a sudden stroke not five minutes after Natalia left his office.

She refused to seek any more outside help. She didn't want to end up locked away in some mental ward. Natalia knew she wasn't crazy. Though the shadows of innocent lives she had taken that constantly surrounded her made it hard for her to stay sane — Liam, two days, hit by a bus.

Carl, one day, mauled by bear.

Alex, died only hours later, plane engine part dislodged from a Boeing at thirty five thousand feet, smacked him right in the head.

Tony, gone the next day, bungee cord snapped as he dove off a waterfall.

There were more, so many more...hundreds. None of the deaths could be traced back to her, but it didn't matter. She knew she killed them. She knew no one could help her.

Though she knew she was just trying to survive, the guilt sometimes became too much for her. Some nights she sat up crying, holding a box cutter to her wrist, wishing for the will to end it. But a part of her was determined to make it, to find a cure. She was hopeful that maybe one day it would just stop. Natalia wasn't ready to give up yet. So she hunted through medical books, internet sites, articles, anything she could get her hands on that might give some clue to her affliction. But she was never able to come up with anything.

Natalia's thoughts drifted to the stranger she had tonight. How she didn't even get his name — better that way. With no identity, he was not real. He might not join the others...*Bullshit. He'll be there. His shadow will be standing with the rest of them.*

Natalia's stomach churned. *The hell with it.* She couldn't eat, she couldn't sleep, she would just drive. She looked up to see the cute boy staring at her. His lips mouthed, "Hi." *I've got to get out of here.*

She threw a ten on the counter and headed out the door. The cute guy's party trailed behind her. She walked up to her car, mishandled and dropped her keys. As she bent to scoop them up, she heard a voice behind her.

"Hey, wanna party?"

He was wearing Drakkar, her favorite. She turned to face him. He swept his sandy-blonde hair out of his deep green eyes. *Stunning.*

"No."

"Come on, come party with us — you like fun, dontchya?"

"There's a bar down the street a few blocks, it's kind of a dive. But, there's really nowhere else to go without hopping on the highway. You boys will have fun there, I'm sure."

"You shouldn't be all by yourself on a Saturday night, baby." He had an adorable, impish grin. His eyes sparkled.

"I'm tired — thanks for the offer though."

"Oh," he grabbed her upper arm, "but I insist." He shoved Natalia against the van as it pulled up behind her. The door yanked open, hands fell upon her, wrestled her into the dark. Someone pinned her to the floor while the cute boy with the impish grin shouted, "Drive!"

Natalia could smell a mixture of oil and cologne. Hands pressed her face to the cold, steel floor. She couldn't see. Someone tied her wrists together, another tied her ankles. A sack was pulled over her head as she was propped against the wall of the van.

It all happened so fast. She tried to picture the faces of the boys at the diner, but the only one she could manifest was the cute boy. They had laughed, talked in hushed tones while they eyeballed her and made fun of the waitress, all the while plotting a gang rape over their banana sundaes. *I'm going to die tonight.* Her body shivered as tears smeared her face.

Someone turned on the stereo, the bass line of some hip-hop band throbbed, matched the pounding of her heart. She cinched her back into the side of the van, trying to steady herself as it swerved around corners at a rapid pace.

She couldn't be sure how much time passed or how far they'd traveled, but it was an eternity before the van came to a stop. She heard the back doors open, again their hands were on her, dragged her out and tossed her to the ground. One of them ripped the hood off her.

There were five of them. The boy closest to her held a knife, moonlight glimmered along the edge of the blade. He walked over to her and cut the rope that bound her ankles.

"If you try to run, or scream, I will slit your throat. Do you understand?" Natalia nodded.

She sat there in the dirt and looked around. It was some sort of deserted construction site, probably condos. She swallowed hard.

Her mind ran through all the men she'd been with, all the lives she'd fucked to death. She had wished for sweet oblivion to release her from this parasitic prison many times. Maybe death was the only answer. And now she wouldn't have to wrestle with it anymore, wouldn't have to contemplate doing it herself.

This is it. This is what I deserve.

She looked up to meet the eyes of the boy with the moonlit blade...she stared through him, her face twisted into a sneer.

The cute boy pushed through to the front, "Me first...and third."

With the sound of his zipper, Natalia began to laugh. She spread her legs wide. "Come and get me motherfuckers! I'm all yours."

What inspired "Hunger"?

"Hunger" was a complete break from the norm for me with how I approach the writing process. I usually have at least a semi-formed idea of what I want the story to be. But this one started with just one sentence that popped in my head out of nowhere. The first line in the original draft of this story was, "Natalia breathed into the stranger's pillow as he fucked her from behind." I had no idea where the story was going, who this woman was, or how it was all going to end. I just kept typing and typing until I hit the end. The version in this anthology, though, is the result of many edits. I'd like to thank m.j euringer, Gary Frank, and Mary SanGiovanni for making it what it is today.

Scopophilia
Peter Gutiérrez

Peter Gutiérrez... wakes up in Montclair on most mornings... kisses two boys goodnight... reads them bedtime stories and adds things that aren't in the text to keep 'em on their toes... has published about ten books, including a handful of comics collections/graphic novels but no prose novels... consults for publishing and media companies... considers himself an educator... writes about and teaches film whenever possible... in comics is most proud of an anthology of Japanese ghost stories done (long ago) for Crusade... occasionally sells short fiction to genre magazines or school/YA collections... watches too many horror movies...sleeps uneasily.

*P*lease know that I make so rude an observation as that which follows only because I have long been a member of the class it assaults. That said, I'm certain the reader will agree that when academics engage in social activities it is usually with a flair both outsized and exceedingly false. These self-congratulatory banquets and garden parties take on a contrived air that would, were it not for the free flow of spirits, be insufferable. It is as though the organizers seek to assure themselves that their community is not the withdrawn, sedentary enclave the world often takes it for.

Clayton and I, therefore, should not have been surprised when we learned that the afternoon's portion of the symposium—entitled "Human and Animal Societies–Recent Findings from the Field"—had been rescheduled in favor of a series of impromptu hunting parties on that blusterous autumn day in the year 1906. "But this is Princeton!" I had protested. "A citadel of higher learning…!"

"Ah," Clayton had said, that redoubtable gleam in his eye, "but only because this institution enjoys such stature do certain liberties avail themselves—and the ability to embrace them without apology when they do. You've heard, Mr. James, of the man-made lake that is nearing completion a mile from where we repose?"

"Of course," I said irritably. This monumental enterprise, which involved the damming of local waterways to flood nearby marshland, was underwritten by that robber-baron-turned-philanthropist Andrew Carnegie; this had in turn prompted the department chair who had invited us to quip that the surface of the water would not gleam blue so much as green.

"But what of this lake, Mr. Pierce?" I continued, rising to Clayton's bait. "Surely the announcement did not specify hunting when in actuality they've gone fishing?"

My partner then graciously explained how the dredging of the mud had rendered homeless much of the native fauna, the armies of horse-drawn wagons in effect flushing the game. Still, such sport held little appeal for us. We had slain beasts on nearly every continent, but usually for reasons related to food— either to attain it or to avoid becoming it. Outside, the sun radiated unseasonable warmth although clouds, drizzle and fierce winds mitigated against the full administration of its effects. In short, it was perfectly dismal: ideal weather for hunting. Or rather, for the subsequent telling of tales about hunting, which is often the prime motive for the activity itself.

In sharp contrast, the library of the Dean of Studies, with its raging fire of fragrant scotch pine, could easily lead one to imagine that mankind had permanently tamed the elements. In point of fact, all such a room represented was a thoroughly modern cave in which to hide; the ultimate fulfillment of the Paleolithic dream, but hardly an advance in aspiration.

Books filled the walls up to the chevron cornices. Their orderly bindings presented a face of learned stability that stood in opposition to the more primeval setting outside the high-thrown casements. The view from these was primarily of a courtyard across which undergraduates scurried, their books beneath their cloaks. Beyond was a stand of trees that, though dense, was not terribly deep: looming over it was a gothic tower not unlike the one in which we were ensconced, as if civilization were encroaching on that little copse from all sides.

The pursuit of such observations was well-served by the library's massive armchairs. Each was accompanied by a side table in teak, the diameters of which had been felicitously designed just wide enough to accommodate a tumbler and an ashtray. Clayton's figure was obscured by the back of his chair as he perused a volume on, I believe, Icelandic botany. Apart from the odd servant, there was but one other gentleman present. Of indeterminate age, he looked ill at ease in his high, starched collar and ascot. Despite his average height I sensed about him a sinewy strength rarely present in scholars. As a pretext for approaching him, I rose from my upholstered seat to study the damp, swirling landscape on the other side of the leaded glass.

His nearly-black hair was an unruliness that had been combed straight back with what I surmised to be a cousin of a horse brush. He had the dusky complexion one associates with the Southern Hemisphere, and it struck me that his foreign origin might account for his being alone. I wanted to assure him that with the presence of Clayton and myself, fellowship was not out of the question. However, I hesitated upon noticing that he was completely enrapt in the vista below.

There a gaunt figure in his shirtsleeves moved through the brambles with the rain falling lightly upon him. Hatless, he had to wipe occasionally at his brow, blinking as he did so. He glanced from side to side, both intently and aimlessly—as if he had lost something and was open to the possibility of its being virtually anywhere.

I addressed the foreigner: "What is he doing, may I ask?"

"The same thing as you and I, sir," he replied in a deep, almost guttural, voice. "Looking."

"Yes," I agreed, "but at what?"

"Who knows?" the foreigner said quietly. He turned to me ever so briefly, as though acknowledging our incipient conversation but also indicating, through the economy of his glance, that he could not take his eyes from the fellow in the briars. "Perhaps the flow of an ant-filled stream. Or a mayfly revolving slowly in a newly-formed puddle."

"The gentleman is a naturalist?" I asked.

"No," came the reply. "He is Gardner Meserve, the photographer."

"Hold on, now," I exclaimed. "*That* is Gardner Meserve!"

Straight away I was mortified by the note of scandalized excitement in my voice. Awkwardly, I tried to transform my tone into one of awe at being in the presence (so to speak) of such a noteworthy personage. In the pages of the Geographic Society's journal he had been quoted as saying that our universe created striking images every moment, that his job was simply to capture as many of these as possible. In keeping with this principle, the Canadian Meserve had recorded with equal sensitivity subjects as diverse as Arab street urchins at play and the thunderous effects of rainy season upon Victoria Falls. Through his work, the world's wonders were brought into staggeringly intimate proximity.

Sadly, it was rumored he had returned from the East last year with—there is no delicate way to put this—an addiction to opium so pronounced that he had forsaken wife and children in the most shameful fashion. Still, I had not been surprised to find his name on this week's list of prize recipients; it represented a chance to honor the man before his further descent into depravity made even that impossible.

Then it struck me. "You're Mr. Neto," I said.

"Manuel Neto, yes," he said, offering me his hand but not his eyes.

I could not recall whether he was from Brazil or rather a Portuguese, his dark skin the result of years of traveling under the sun as Meserve's aide-de-camp. Their partnership was not too different from how I liked to imagine Clayton's and mine was perceived: the maverick who owes much of his success to the steadiness of his right hand.

"I am Carter James," I said. "Without undue modesty, I am certain that—"

The interruption at this point did not stem from Neto, but rather from the sight that assailed me from outdoors. Meserve was looking toward the heavens, his countenance plainly visible. At once the biologist in me suspected that the palsy I beheld was due to an affliction of the nervous system, perhaps parasitical in origin; for although the rain had now ceased, the man would not stop blinking. It was not the quick twitch of one whose eyes have been offended by some passing mote, nor the slow, deliberate closing of fatigue. Rather, it was a light, pulsing movement that required minimal exertion and which for some reason I found vaguely unnerving.

"Do you know…?"

Misunderstanding me, perhaps intentionally, Neto said, "The clouds most likely. At the shadows they cast through the atmosphere."

I craned my neck to confirm this, but it was an impossible angle. To cover my frustration, I asked the obvious—why Neto was not by his side. When he answered, it was with the air of a man sharing a confidence. "Mr. Meserve values his privacy. To have me about constantly would be… burdensome."

As politely as possible, I pointed out to my new acquaintance that he was, in fact, spying on Meserve.

"Pardon me, Mr. James, but he knows quite well I am watching: he is my charge. You see, he cannot afford any mishap that would have him close his eyes."

Neto was clearly speaking metaphorically, implying that Meserve could never rest, so great was his obsession with the visual. The entire incident then began to strike me as artificial—the great *artiste* wandering in the mist while his faithful assistant keeps a gloomy vigil. Were these the ingredients that they would use to perpetuate a romantic version of Meserve's reputation?

"Very good, then," I said smartly. "It was a pleasure meeting you, Mr. Neto."

By way of reply, he did something wholly unexpected: he fastened his eyes on me. It was a terrible look, not in terms of affect, but in intensity, possessing a frankness people do not often employ even on their deathbeds. Indeed, his eyes seemed out of place in the face of so well-spoken a man—nay, any man.

The heat and grip of Neto's hand on my forearm commanded the portion of me not already under the thrall of his eyes. "I desire that you hear the entire story, Mr. James. For I know of your work, too, and believe you may regard our experience without prejudice."

Forcing a smile, I reached down to remove Neto's grasp from my person... but his hands were clasped behind his back. Rubbing the spot where the palpable sensation had occurred, I consented rather lamely: "Well, it is a dreary day—when better to hear so dreadful a tale?"

"Oh, not dreadful, Mr. James. *Awful*."

Turning abruptly, I signaled for tea to the white-gloved attendants while also assuring myself of Clayton's continued presence, proof of which was provided by the stream of smoke pluming languidly over the top of his chair as Neto launched into his story.

*

Meserve had been invited by the Secretary of the Interior for the Philippine insular government, Dean Conant Worcester, to record the primitive practices of the Kalinga in remote areas of the island chain. Properly speaking, no such people exist, *Kalinga* deriving from the native word for "constant warfare" and designating a variety of separate tribes. This definition should help illustrate American intentions in the region, *pacification* being the key watchword. Moreover, attacks from the more intractable of these clans could not be permitted to interfere with the extraction of the gold deposits thought to lie in the mountains. Worcester's plan was to replicate the stratagem Britain had used elsewhere—to marshal financial and political interests by appealing to Christian virtues. The Kalinga would be dealt with not by brute subjugation, but as the outcome of an ostensibly humanitarian cause.

Despite such dubious aims, Meserve was quick to realize the advantages of accompanying well-funded Americans into what was largely unexplored territory. To Neto, though, he confided the hope that his work would have the opposite effect, namely, of increasing interest in the preservation of the indigenous cultures. He had no desire simply to add to the voyeuristic documentation of bare-breasted women, filed teeth, and similar images that constituted Worcester's chief interest. Meserve's contention, born not so much from noble motives as aesthetic, was that if we treat primitives with respect, they will show us how to perceive nature in ways that we have "forgotten."

After a fortnight living amongst the lowland Kalinga, he became restless. Not that these people weren't fascinating—with their casual diet of ants, their sprawling tattoos—but his voracious eye had eaten its full and wanted more. Through their Tagalog interpreter, he and Neto heard tantalizing legends concerning the "Shadow-Eaters" of the highlands. Among these was the claim that they could transform themselves into rats or bears—even members of other Kalinga tribes—in order to evade detection by white men.

Worcester's representative in camp could only substantiate a more mundane, if tragic, aspect of these same apocrypha: the Shadow-Eaters had recently massacred a cadre of surveyors in the hills and, consistent with the ghastly local tradition, taken their heads as trophies. Indeed, because of the danger they posed, Worcester had left specific instructions to discourage Meserve from seeking them out—and were he to insist, to make sure it was in the company of an armed contingent. The Canadian could only smile, as he knew that the presence of soldiers would spell certain doom. Worcester's man, shrugging at Meserve's fateful decision, then produced a powdery medicine to safeguard against the local fevers that had so devastated Spanish forces on their jungle campaigns.

And so the two adventurers set off, ascending into the hills with a water buffalo, a single revolver, and no interpreter. After a matter of hours the treacherously muddy carriage roads disappeared, and they were forced to hack their own path. Only the fatigue of this march enabled them to sleep at night, given the unseen presence of the monkeys; one could never be certain their cries were not the cunning mimicry of men in the trees. Matters worsened when, as an unintended effect of the medicine, both began to develop a mild, but nagging cough.

On the slope of an inactive volcano they came upon a trail of headless remains, made up mainly, but not solely, of animals. As if forming a chronological record of bloodthirstiness, each skeleton was less fully decomposed than the previous. At the trailhead, near a modest, vine-covered rockface that unpleasantly resembled hair on a scalp, were corpses in Western dress. The cave thus concealed was clearly the site of the butchery, the remains unceremoniously deposited in front only to have gravity and rainfall persuade them down the slope. To Meserve, this burial practice, or lack thereof, was nothing short of astounding given most primitive people's fear of the dead. Neto, by contrast, had no time for such elevated thoughts. He knew they were being watched.

*

At this point, I became acutely aware of a chill that had permeated the windows. The final ounce of Prince of Wales in my hand was now as cold as the china cup in which it rested. I considered retreating a step towards the fire, but it had died down to a weak crackling.

As Neto's account continued, I reminded myself that we were in a quiet town in central New Jersey; that the familiar aroma of tobacco wafting from Clayton's chair was a sign that Reason still held sway.

*

Possessing the stronger mental constitution of the two, Neto had been entrusted with the revolver. Were all else to fail, they would have recourse to use it—on themselves. So while Meserve began to array photographic prints from his rucksack, Neto made no move for the Colt. And when Meserve was done forming a wide circle of photos atop a bed of glossy jungle leaves and withered bones, Neto joined him to sit sedately at its center.

Then, from their hiding places in the brush, out came the Shadow-Eaters to inspect sights which were beyond their ability to conceive: African "monsters" lumbering across the savanna, Nordic types in alpine settings, the "Grand Canyon" of the American West, a music hall performance in Queensland. To vouch for the veracity of such fantasical images, Meserve also provided subject matter closer to hand—a Sumatran jungle canopy similar to their own and portraits of several lowland Kalinga.

The Shadow-Eaters much resembled the latter. Their canines, though, were not sharpened, perhaps because they had no need to appear fearsome—they were fearsome. Indeed, even the women and children sported axes on bone-linked belts, and encrusted tufts of hair were visible on many of these. Most remarkable, though, was an axe so massive that its head was like a cross-section of a small boulder. The warrior who held it was aided by another who stood behind him so that a second pair of arms appeared at waist-level, as if in imitation of a Hindu icon. Such an arrangement was hardly practical for hunting or warfare, Neto realized, until he saw that its purpose was unrelated to either. Simply letting the weight of this axe drop for a few inches would be sufficient to sever a head as readily as a cleaver might slice a boiled carrot.

Crowding around the photos but hesitant to touch them, the Shadow-Eaters commenced mumbling to each other. Theirs was a tongue full of violent glottal sounds, but uttered softly, presumably so as not to engage the hearing of prey. For several tense moments,

Meserve was unsure about the wisdom of his gambit for he knew that some primitives failed to comprehend the nature of realistic pictorial representations altogether. Fortunately, it was soon clear that the Shadow-Eaters were thoroughly impressed with the sorcery by which their Western guests had transformed their photographic subjects into two-dimensions...

Upon casual inspection one would be unaware that the Shadow-Eaters lived in the cave, so hidden were their sleeping quarters. They had dug narrow pits in the volcanic soil into which they lowered themselves; though there was evidence of charcoal at the bottom of these, the cave was miraculously free of the odor of fire. More perplexing was the source of the food itself because while there appeared to be no organized hunting excursions, fresh meat—forest pig, monkey, and all manner of tropical birds—was always at hand. To Neto, this phenomenon explained the Shadow-Eaters' name: puzzled as to what nourishment the tribe survived upon, outsiders had speculated that they devoured the darkness itself.

One night the two friends awakened to the *pat-pat* of animal paws from the cave floor above. They pulled themselves up on vine-ropes to peer over the edge of their pit. A species of pygmy deer wandered deeper into the cave and promptly tumbled into a neighboring hole. Instantly a squeal went up as the poor beast was set upon by the ever-present axes. To the amazement of both men, a jungle fowl with loping tail feathers then strutted inside and, evading the pits by the sheerest of luck, continued back into the vast darkness. What lured the wildlife was not apparent, for there were neither baited traps within nor foul weather without to account for these incursions.

Soon afterwards they accompanied the chieftain and several warriors on their daily trip into the deeper parts of the cave to learn whether a water or food source lay therein. Prohibited the use of torches, Meserve and Neto groped pathetically through the stygian darkness in which the natives seemed so at home. In time an unexpected boon came in the form of a faint, phosphorous-like luminescence that coated the walls and allowed one's eyes to take in the cavernous terrain. "You see what this means?" Meserve whispered, and indeed Neto did: this unconventional light source turned the surroundings into a natural darkroom.

When they came to a flat, shoulder-high pedestal of rock their escort halted abruptly and deposited the head of the pygmy deer. Immediately Meserve scooped it into his sack and indicated that they would bring it in person to whomever this offering was intended. As he and Neto were esteemed to be mighty sorcerers, this wish was indulged.

Neto, though not surrendering to fear, harbored grave doubts about journeying where headhunters dared not. Meserve, his face alive with passion as he patted his camera in the blackness, would not be deterred. What wonders would they see that no other men, civilized or savage, had ever laid eyes upon?

They were perhaps a mile from the surface when they heard the delayed echoes of their own words. "What wonders..." came Meserve's voice. "What wonders...."

But then they saw him, the tribal medicine man perched atop a mound of skins. From his silhouette came the cadence of their own Western voices. In his hands, he shook a desiccated but unmistakably human ear; at his feet were the feathers of the jungle fowl he had just consumed.

Suddenly both men grasped why they had come
here against all good sense: they had been summoned.

*

Forgive the editorial intrusion, but I have always
found the descriptor "medicine man" to carry an
unwelcome pharmaceutical connotation; I use it here
because Neto did. The term "witch doctor," now largely
out of favor, seems more apropos given the diabolical
nature of the individual in question—as will presently
be detailed.

*

The medicine man never left the recesses of the
cave, and to gaze upon him in daylight was taboo. The
Shadow-Eaters' trophy-taking was done to placate him
as he used the heads for various rituals, usually
removing their brains from their cases. I hesitate to
relate this next nauseating item, but he cooked these in
a kind of stew in large ceramic pots. These were heated
smokelessly, for they were now so far inside the
volcano that geothermal vents were commonplace. The
foulest of fumes emanated from these cauldrons, and
the medicine man inhaled them deeply. By this obscure
form of sympathetic magic, he was able to reproduce
the sounds, smells, and mannerisms of other beings,
thus providing a basis for the shape-changing legends.

Understandably wary, each guest took turns keeping
watch with the revolver while the other slept. Their
anxiety was ill-founded, though, as their host was filled
with curiosity about their own magic. To avoid
disappointing him, Meserve used his lighting apparatus
to take photos of the cavern, careful not to aim his lens
at the medicine man. At every flash of the bulb, he
jumped with glee, a response that only intensified when
Meserve used groundwater and his "darkroom" to
develop the prints.

In return, the medicine man revealed a horde of skulls that he had organized much like a curator. This cultural exchange seemed to vindicate Meserve's original theory: they had arrived open-minded and respectful, and so were greeted in the same spirit. Indeed, everything was as idyllic as one could expect in the company of a bat-like, brain-cooking sorcerer. That is, until the daily offerings stopped appearing on the rock-altar...

After hours at his steaming cauldrons yielded no change, the medicine man journeyed swiftly back to the cave mouth to learn what was the matter. As there was no point staying behind in the dark, Meserve and Neto followed. When they emerged in the moonlight, there was only devastation and the medicine man howling in impotent rage. During their absence the tribe had succumbed to the common cold from which their visitors had long since recovered. Down to the last child, its members were wheezing their final breaths or had already done so. So much for the super-human Shadow-Eaters, Meserve remarked to Neto—felled by the most human of ailments!

The medicine man wept openly, shaking his talismans and gnashing his teeth—and that is the last thing Neto recalled of the scene.

For when he next opened his eyes it was daylight and he was buried up to his neck in the bottom of a newly-dug pit. It took a moment for him to realize that his arms were pinned to his sides not by soil, but by the weight of the tribe's dead, which had been piled around him. From nearby came an inhuman howling. It was Meserve, in his own pit.

Attracted by the carrion, rats and vultures soon descended and found Neto's head an appetizing side dish to the rotting flesh. Helpless, Neto had to lash out with his teeth at the beasts—in effect a savage himself now. In his pocket was the Colt, but he could not reach it. All he could do was scream and scream, hoping that rain would not wash mud into the putrid hole and drown him. To this day his voice had not fully recovered, but was instead a dry, cracked-sounding thing.

Next followed the only happy miracle of the entire adventure. By pure chance a group of missionaries, themselves lost on their way to meet an assembly of *pangats*, the Kalinga's elder statesmen, stumbled across our heroes. Neto was barely alive while Meserve was in the throes of total hysteria—and blinking incessantly. Between their two pits lay the naked corpse of the medicine man, except for his head, which some foraging animal had made off with. His legs had apparently lifted the great axe, the sacrifice of his own skull consecrating his final and most powerful act of sorcery: the punishment of he who had decimated his people. For this was indeed the task Meserve had accomplished, having been unwittingly assigned it by Worcester and his "medicine."

Beheading himself and torturing Neto—even such excesses paled when compared to the curse visited upon Meserve. The photographer had made the mistake of carrying images of his family on his person and these were the materials that the devil used to haunt all his waking moments. For when Meserve closed his eyes, he was beset by the most horrible vision—his two beautiful children ripped to pieces, as if subjected to the Shadow-Eaters' mighty axes.

But that was not all; the fiend had added another component to the curse. When Meserve's eyes were open, he saw the world through the lens of his beloved wife similarly hacked. In order to deny these hellish visions from manifesting fully, the poor fellow had to alternate rapidly between the two, his only respite lying in that instant when one image replaced the other and neither was clear.

Thus his estrangement from his family was explained: their presence made the psychological pain of his torments that much greater. By the time Neto finished, I understood too the reason behind Meserve's opium habit—the drug enabling him to pass swiftly into the haven that was unconsciousness. For a man in love with looking, this condition was no less than damnation. And although such comparisons are facile, his curse was surely worse than blindness: the blind can use the mind's eye to conjure the world in peace, a pleasure forever denied Meserve, who, it must be said, had had his gaze utterly broken.

*

Neto had not removed his eyes from Meserve, and I had not taken mine from him. Other than placing his hands in his pockets to warm them, he had not moved.

I, in contrast, moved frantically towards Clayton, so eager was I to hear a rational explanation for the story just concluded. To my horror, though, my friend was not in his chair—

When I turned to face Neto, thankfully Clayton was at his back, which meant that he had just been behind me. I had no time to marvel at his stealth, though, as Neto was presently adding a postscript: "...and since the photographs were left in the cave, we lack proof. That is why I cannot expect people to believe our account."

"I beg to differ," Clayton said loudly. "The public ought not believe your account because it is dishonest on one essential matter."

~100~

"I do not follow, sir," replied Neto calmly, pivoting to face his accuser. "Moreover, you'll forgive me, both of you, but Gardner is coming inside..."

"Of course he's coming inside!" Clayton shouted. "You called him just as you did the missionaries. 'Miracle' indeed! What do you take us for?" Then to me: "His hands, Carter. Recall how he commanded his victims from a distance."

I could not respond. It was as though a magnetized rod had brushed the length of my back, causing each hair to stand on end.

The foreigner's eyes were now blazing. "You'll regret how you slander me, Mr. Pierce!"

Clayton merely chuckled and took a step forward. "Then prove me wrong by emptying your pockets. Or remove your old-fashioned collar and show us that it does not conceal the tattoos on your neck!"

"My God, Clayton, what are you saying?"

"I think you know, Carter. He may have a face and voice like that of the late Manuel Neto, but this man was no more born in Lisbon than you or I. His 'recovering' larynx is merely the excuse he uses while his mind continues to assimilate the speech patterns contained in Neto's brain—"

And then the most extraordinary thing happened. Hopping briskly onto one of the side tables, our storyteller threw open the casement and—leaped into the wind.

Clayton whirled, barking to the attendants. "Inform the proctors at once! There's a madman at large on the campus." He paused and then, looking down from the open window, added, "And another who requires medical care."

I felt a third was about to join their number unless I could make events conform to Reason. "Tell me, why on earth would the medicine man leave his homeland to undertake this elaborate masquerade?"

"Why not, Carter? His people dead, how could he survive on his own? Or hope to escape Worcester's colonial justice? More positively, now he can see firsthand the world that so captivated him in Meserve's photos."

"That makes sense—to a point. For how could Meserve himself not know his trusted companion?"

"Your question has merit, Carter," he said thoughtfully. "With your pardon, may I venture that he has never really gotten a good look at him?"

I glanced at Clayton sharply and caught what seemed to be a sardonic smile. It is difficult to say, though, for the glimpse was fleeting: Clayton was already in the comfortable arms of an overstuffed chair by the fire, which was once again at a roar.

What inspired "Scopophilia"?

I've written about the two framing characters—Pierce and James—before, and always wanted to do so again. They first appeared in a dark fantasy set in the Old West that was commissioned by a themed anthology in the late '90s. I have a bunch of other yarns planned for them—ones in which they won't be quite so passive as they are here. As for the rest of the story elements, inclusion in this anthology dictated a New Jersey setting. Princeton naturally sprang to mind. It's a location I'm comfortable using, having misspent several years of my youth there.

As for the story's deeper issues, they're more personal and it's harder to articulate where they came from. In any case, they'd been banging around my head, and then I got the idea of wedding them to a Pierce and James story. The notion of using the Philippines was suggested by a book I wrote on East Asian music/culture in the fall of 2006. Then, as I began research for "Scopophilia," other items fell into place. For example, I learned it was the 100th anniversary of Lake Carnegie, so it seemed like a good idea to include it somehow. (By the way, many of the dates, locations, events and proper names that relate to the American colonial experience in the Philippines are accurate in terms of the historical record.)

Family First
J.G. Faherty

J.G. Faherty has had a varied career, which provides a rich background for his writing. Currently a successful resume and educational writer, his previous jobs have included laboratory manager, R&D scientist, accident scene/fashion photographer, zoo keeper, salesman, cook, advice columnist, and anatomy instructor.

J.G. began writing horror/dark fiction in 2003. His fiction and poetry have appeared in numerous anthologies, magazines, and e-zines, and his children's fiction has been published in educational books and online by The Princeton Review and other academic publishing houses. He has regular columns in the Horror Writers Association newsletter and several horror-related websites. His most recent fiction credits include Cemetery Dance and the Bound for Evil anthology.

You can visit him at www.jgfaherty.com.

*I*ntense pain filled the man's head. He couldn't think clearly. He tried to focus but a burning hunger filled him, obliterating all other thoughts.

Where am I? Woods, trees. Daylight. This is all wrong. I was in my car. Driving... Those people, in the road...

Teeth, biting...blood.

The rest disappeared into a hazy, black cloud. When it cleared, new thoughts came to him.

Wait...my name is John. I have a family. A wife. Sheila. She's blonde. The children...

The ground slanted in front of him, causing him to lose his balance.

Must climb, go home. Find my family. One hand in the ground, then the other. Move my feet.

I can do this.

He reached the top of the hill. A car sat there, the door open, the windows broken.

My car? Was there an accident?

Why didn't anyone find me?

Walk, must walk. Someone will see me. Find me.

He took one step and then another. It was hard to move his feet, as if they didn't want to obey.

So hungry. It hurts, hurts inside. Need a hospital.

Need food.

The sound of an approaching truck broke the stillness. The tractor trailer came to a stop in a squeal of airbrakes.

He tried to speak to the man climbing out of the cab.

"I...I...help..."

The sudden smell of food overwhelmed him, pushed away all other thoughts.

Food. Must eat. Must...

Oh, God, no! I...
Must eat.

*

"Mom, why can't we leave? Everyone else is gone." Bobby Grainger set down his binoculars and turned his piercing blue eyes, so much like his father's, towards his mother.

"You know why, sweetie. It's too dangerous. Those things are out there. There's no place for us to go." Sheila ran a hand through her hair, smoothing it back from her face. Her hand came away greasy. It'd been four days since the dead rose up. Since then, the closest she'd come to bathing had been washing her hands and face at the kitchen sink.

There was no way she was leaving Bobby and Stacie alone, not even for ten minutes. And at ages nine and eleven, they refused to stay in the bathroom with her, or bathe together.

She knew the severity of the situation hadn't sunk into their MTV-trained attention spans. To them this was something new, something exciting, not a life-threatening catastrophe.

Not yet.

It would take them a while to realize television, school, their friends, the mall, all those things might be gone for a long time to come.

Maybe forever.

"There're zombies here, too, Mom," Bobby said, using the one word she hated to hear. "Maybe we could drive into the city, find the police. Or go deep into the woods, to a cabin or something."

Sheila shook her head. "No. All the cities, from Princeton to Manhattan, are full of them. Don't you remember the news before the TV went out?

And we don't know what's in the woods. They could be there, too."

"Besides, dorkwad, you don't know the first thing about camping. You couldn't start a fire with matches and gasoline." Stacie, her dark blonde hair still streaked with pale yellow from their vacation at Seaside last month, gave her younger brother the kind of smug look pre-teens seem to develop from nowhere.

"Oh, yeah? Well you..."

"Enough, both of you." Sheila used what her kids called 'the tone.' Four days stuck in the house with her two children and they were already on each others' nerves.

For the thousandth time she wished John was here with them. He had a way of saying just the right thing, a funny, off-the-cuff comment or a calming word, to diffuse almost any situation.

He'd gone missing the same day the dead began rising from their graves. He'd been working late - she hadn't expected him back 'til after midnight - so it wasn't until morning that she'd realized he'd never made it home.

By then, the police had their hands full and weren't even answering the phones, let alone looking into missing persons cases.

Every time she thought about him, a reluctant acceptance of his death struggled with the hope that he'd gotten off the turnpike and found a place to hide, a motel or office building, and that he was alive.

And if he was alive, she knew he'd find a way back to them. That was the real reason they weren't leaving. But she couldn't broach that subject with Stacie and Bobby.

It wouldn't be fair to get their hopes up.

Not when the chances were so small.

*

John Grainger looked down at himself.

God help me, I did it.

The memories had returned, his thought process almost normal. As if...

As if the flesh and blood restored them.

He wiped his hands on his torn and filthy shirt, leaving red smears, strings of skin and tissue, and pink gobs of brain.

He'd devoured the man from the truck. Torn his throat out. Clawed into him until he reached the softest parts, the juiciest tidbits.

His mind had screamed in horrified disgust but something else had control.

The craving.

The human meat had tasted better, more satisfying, than any meal he'd ever eaten in his life.

And it had restored him.

I'm a monster.

But was he? Maybe it was only this one time; maybe the human flesh had returned his sanity, his 'self.'

I need to get back to Sheila and the kids. They'll be worried. Have to make sure they're safe, then they can get me to a hospital, a research lab. Someplace where they can study me, find a cure.

Return me to normal.

John stepped over the remains of the driver and looked inside. The oversized gear lever and confusing array of buttons and gauges convinced him he'd be better off walking.

Home. Have to get home.

John headed north on the Turnpike towards Fort Lee.

Towards home.

*

"Mom, I see something."

Sheila hurried over to the front window, alarmed by the quiver in her daughter's voice. It had been three days since the last creature approached their cul-de-sac, let alone came near their house. One of the neighbors had shot that one, just before he'd packed his whole family into their Denali and taken off for God knows where.

The body still lay on the sidewalk, a bloated sack of putrefying flesh after seventy-two hours in the hot, muggy July weather.

It's like a giant version of a dead woodchuck, she thought, barely able to contain a sudden insane giggle.

Now isn't the time to lose it. Get a grip.

She moved Stacie aside and peeked out the window. Sure enough, something was moving at the far end of the street where it branched off from Culver Avenue, right by the Henderson's house.

"Bobby, give me the binoculars." The sudden magnification made it seem as if she'd leaped down the street.

The person was dead, no doubt about that. The herky-jerky movements, the shuffling feet, the dirty, torn clothes covered in blood.

Sheila's stomach did a flip-flop, threatening to release the tomato soup she'd had for lunch. She closed her eyes and concentrated on keeping the food down.

They didn't have enough to spare to waste it on being squeamish.

When she had herself under control, she opened her eyes. The thing - *zombie, dammit. Call it what it is* - had turned away and was now walking towards the Henderson's front door.

She realized the Henderson's car was still in the driveway. Were they still home, hiding out the same way she had her family hidden here?

The zombie stopped and tilted its head, turning first one way and then the other. She couldn't see its face but it looked as if the creature was sniffing at something.

Smelling for food? Can they do that?

"Bobby, Stacie. Shut all the windows in the house. Hurry."

"But Mom, it's hot out. If we shut the windows..."

"Goddammit, Bobby, shut up and do what I say!" She kept her voice low, not shouting. If the things could smell people they sure as hell could hear them.

Footsteps behind her let her know the kids had gone off to do what she'd told them. She'd explain later. She pulled down the windows nearest to her, the ones on either side of the front door, and closed the gauzy, blue curtains as well.

She pushed aside the material just enough to aim the binoculars out.

The undead man had moved again. She managed to catch a glimpse of his leg as he went around the side of the house, heading for the Henderson's back yard.

She watched him open the gate, realized they couldn't be as mindless as the news said. *Theirs is funny. It sticks. You have to jiggle the latch and pull up on the gate at the same time. Unless you knew that you could stand there forever trying to open it.*

The kids came back down the stairs, Bobby's sneakers thump-thumping on the wood. The way his feet grew, he'd soon need another pair.

Doesn't look like we'll be shopping anytime in the near future. By now the Paramus Park and Garden State malls must look like something from Dawn of the Dead.

Hell, we might all *be barefoot by winter.*

If we're still alive.

That last thought was a black crow that circled endlessly through the landscape of her thoughts. She'd catch sight of it during the day, sometimes far away, sometimes close by. At night it roosted right over her as she lay on the bed, Bobby and Stacie sleeping on either side of her.

"Mom, can I have something to drink? I'm thirsty."

You think you're thirsty now? Wait until the water's shut off and we're living on what falls from the sky, she wanted to shout at him, but John's face appeared, telling her to stay calm.

They're just kids, he would have said. *You're the adult. Act like it.*

As long as the water's working let them drink all they need.

"Go ahead. In fact, let's all go get one."

*

I'm a monster.

John couldn't deny it any longer. He stood in the Henderson's living room, which resembled a charnel house more than the relaxed, classically-decorated space it had been before he'd arrived. The last thing he remembered was opening the gate, the one that stuck all the time.

When his awareness returned he'd been standing over Tom Henderson's body, his mouth full of blood and tissue and loops of intestines around his hands, their other end still attached to Tom's body.

Puddles of blood soaked into the Persian rug; more splattered across the walls and furniture.

And the taste – oh Lord, the exquisite, wonderful flavor!

A gaping hole in Tom's abdomen revealed where the delicious bounty had originated. Chunks of brownish-red liver lay strewn around the floor.

From where he stood, John could see into the kitchen. Enid Henderson lay on the linoleum, her gray-haired skull shattered and empty. A brick lay beside her, which he must have used to crack open her head like a walnut.

All to satisfy his unholy lust, his craving, for human flesh.

"Jesus Christ." It came out as garbled moan.

The past three days had been spent alternating between cloudy awareness and bestial savagery. Walking the Turnpike. Scavenging among the corpses in their cars.

But now his head was clear.

He remembered why he was here.

Bobby. Stacie.

Sheila.

He had to get them somewhere safe, away from the monsters.

Monsters like him.

John closed his eyes, tried to block out the explosion of gore surrounding him. There had to be a way to be around his family without losing control.

A shadow moved past one of the front windows.

He walked to the front door, peered outside. Three men staggered down the center of the street, heading towards the far end of the cul-de-sac.

Towards his house.

Quietly, slowly, he eased the door open. From the small front porch he could see to the end of the road. There was movement in one of the windows of his house, a twitch as a curtain fell back in place. *Sheila and the kids. They're still alive. And those things – things like me – are heading towards them. But how can I save them? I can't even trust myself around them. What if I get hungry again?* Images of his wife and children torn apart to feed his unnatural appetite filled his head.

No!

He turned away and was immediately confronted with the abattoir he'd created. Even now, with his stomach filled to bursting, the sight and scent of the bloody organs sparked a hunger in him.

Wait. That's it!

He knelt down by Tom Henderson's corpse and started stuffing pieces of intestine and other organs into the pockets of his gore-crusted pants. From a closet he took one of Tom's jackets and put it on, filled those pockets as well.

The only way to keep from becoming a dangerous, crazed monster like those things outside was to keep his stomach filled. And if that's what it took to save his family, by God he'd do it.

He chewed and swallowed two big pieces of Enid's liver and then ran out the back door. This time he didn't bother with the gate. Instead, he crashed through the hedges separating the Henderson's property from the Thompson's. From one backyard to the next, dodging lawn furniture and swimming pools, he made his way towards his family.

I'll show them I'm not a monster.

*

Sheila watched the three zombies shambling down the street and knew her family was in trouble. They hadn't looked at any of the other houses; in fact, from the moment they'd appeared they'd been staring in their blank, malevolent way at only one home.

Hers.

Damn John. Why couldn't he have owned a gun?

Why couldn't he be here now to protect them?

"Bobby. Go get your sister's baseball bat."

The fact that he didn't ask any questions, just took off at a run for his room, let her know the seriousness of the situation must have finally sunk in.

"Mom?" Stacie stood by the other window. "There's more coming."

Sheila looked past the three approaching in their lumbering but steady fashion and saw that her daughter was right. More of the creatures were visible at the end of the road, their heads and shoulders cresting the top of the hill where Turtle Dove and Culver split. Six of them, maybe more.

Bobby returned with the bat.

"Go down to the basement and hide," she told them in her best no-nonsense voice, the one she only used when they were in the worst of trouble.

"What about-?"

"Just go! I'll be fine."

She grabbed each of them and gave them a hard kiss, then pushed them towards the kitchen. As she turned back to the window, a flash of movement behind the Pasternack's house caught her eye, but when she looked nothing was there.

Too fast to be one of them. Must have been a cat or something.

The first three zombies – the word came so much easier now that she'd accepted her fate – were only two houses away. Close enough to see their green-brown rotting skin and the way their sunken eyes and open mouths gave them a death's head appearance. One of them wore the remains of a white lab coat with Pascack Valley Hospital stitched on the breast pocket; the other two were naked, with giant 'Y'-shaped autopsy incisions on their chests.

The squeal of tires from of the Pasternack's driveway startled her so badly she dropped the aluminum bat and felt a sharp pain in her chest as her heart gave an extra kick. The lime-green Cadillac roared down the driveway and into the three reanimated corpses, sending them into the air like human bowling pins. The car skidded to a stop and then backed up, crushing the skull of one naked zombie and sending grayish matter flying across the blacktop.

The driver leaned out the window and time seemed to freeze for Sheila.

John!

Then he ducked back into the car, turned it around, and gunned the engine, aiming the heavy vehicle right at the large group of walking dead further up the street.

He's alive!

Then, on the heels of that thought, the image of his face came back to her. The pale flesh, the dark hollows under his eyes.

No. It's impossible. He can't be one of them.

She watched the car drive over the dozen or so zombies at the beginning of the circle. John piloted the car back and forth, a neon-green shark feasting on trapped seals.

None of the zombies attempted to avoid being struck, further evidence in Sheila's mind that none of them had enough brain power to start a car, let alone drive one.

That meant John had to be alive. Hurt, maybe. Tired, exhausted, even sick.

But alive.

With the final zombie dealt with, the car turned and came back down the road at a more sedate pace. Without warning it swerved and struck a mailbox, coming to rest halfway across a front lawn. The driver's door opened and John staggered out, his movements uncoordinated and slow. Even from three houses away she could see blood covering his clothes.

Oh, God, he's hurt. She grabbed the binoculars and hurriedly focused on her husband.

Just in time to see him pull something that looked like a giant pink sponge from his pocket and shove it into his mouth. Gobs of the strange material fell onto his shirt as he chewed and gulped like a starving man who'd just found a steak.

Her stomach did a slow somersault as the hammer of truth struck her.

John, her John, was gone. Replaced by something that shouldn't even be possible.

As she watched, the man who had once been her husband shoved the remains of the unidentifiable organ into one pocket, straightened up, wiped his arm across his mouth, and began walking in a normal fashion towards the house.

What the hell's going on?

A crash from the kitchen interrupted her thoughts. Turning around, she found a fat woman with one arm climbing through the broken glass of the patio door. Two more of the undead waited behind her.

"John!" The unintentional scream burst from her. Without looking to see if he'd heard, she picked up the aluminum bat and prepared to defend her home.

*

John Grainger knew Sheila had seen him. He was too far away to tell what her expression had been, but there was no mistaking the flash of blonde hair as she turned away from the window. Hopefully she'd noticed how he'd taken care of the monsters, that he wasn't like the others.

"John!"

Sheila's voice. Something was wrong. He sprinted for the house, slammed his shoulder into the front door. There was no pain, just a loud crash as the door pulled from its hinges and fell to the floor. He looked around the living room but she wasn't there.

Glass broke in another room. *The kitchen.*

He hurried across the room.

*

The bat hit the dead woman's head with the same sound as when Stacie connected with a softball. The corpse's face caved in on one side and her jaw hung at an angle, but the single hand still reached forward. Behind the woman the other two zombies entered through the shattered door.

She tried to swing again but the bat struck the wall, throwing her aim off.

"Mom?" Bobby shouted from the top of the stairs.

She leaned against the door. "Stay there! Don't come out!" With one hand she pushed the button to lock the door.

Something heavy hit her, knocking her to the floor. At the same time, a sharp pain exploded between her neck and shoulder. She shoved the end of the bat under the dead woman's head and pushed. The creature fell back, blood and green slime running from its mouth. Sheila looked at her shoulder; a piece of skin the size of her fist was missing.

The zombie swallowed and leaned in for another bite. Sheila brought the bat up again but the woman was too heavy; despite only having one arm, her extra strength forced the bat down towards Sheila's neck.

Then the weight was gone.

Shelia sat up and saw her attacker struggling with someone in an ugly brown jacket.

John!

Her husband grabbed the woman's misshapen head with both hands and pulled. The entire thing came free, tearing from the neck in a staccato series of snapping bones. Without pausing, John put his shoulder into the next zombie, an old man in blue pajamas, and knocked him into the teenage zombie. All three of them went down but John rose almost immediately, moving just as fast as she'd seen him do on the racquetball courts for so many years. He grabbed a carving knife from the butcher block and stabbed each of the monsters in the eye. The damaged orbs collapsed inward and stinking yellow fluids gushed out.

The zombies collapsed. Neither rose.

Dropping the knife, John turned to her. "Are you all right?"

She started to answer, but then the room seemed to swim.

Everything went black.

*

John carried his wife into the living room. He heard the children shouting and pounding at the door, but for now Sheila occupied his thoughts.

He laid her on the couch and tore her blouse away,

exposing the damage done by the zombie's teeth. Blood still oozed from the wound. Staring at it, he found himself wanting to put his mouth to it, to taste the blood, feel the flesh against his teeth, tear her open with-

No!

Backing away, he dug pieces of intestine from his pockets and gulped them down. In a moment, the feeling passed and he was able to touch his wife without thinking of her as food.

Her eyes opened.

"John?"

"It's me, honey. I'm here."

"But you're..."

He nodded. "I don't remember how it happened. But I'm okay, as long as I..." He stopped, unable to tell her that the only way he could remain human was with a constant supply of human flesh.

"One of them bit me." Tears welled in her eyes as she said it.

He held her hand. They both knew what it meant; the only question was how long before she turned.

"Will I be like them or you?"

He smiled. "No, I'll make sure you're like me. We'll do what we have to. I won't lose you."

She started to reply but her eyes closed and her head fell back onto the pillow. He touched her neck. No pulse.

She'll be hungry when she wakes up. Have to keep the kids safe from her.

Only one way. Now, before his own hunger came back.

The monsters don't eat their own kind.

He went to the cellar door. "Bobby? Stacie? It's me, Dad."

"Dad?" Their voices, so eager, so innocent.

It's for the best. After, I'll bring them food. Hopefully they'll understand why I had to do it.

"I'm opening the door. Everything's going to be fine."

What inspired "Family First"?

My initial idea for "Family First" came from the same place as all my other zombie stories - I hate the idea that zombies have to be those shuffling, shambling, brainless automatons of the Romero films - not that they're bad, but they could be so much more as well. So I purposely try to create different types of zombies in each story - some are smarter than others, some are created by different means, and some are indistinguishable from living people.

In "Family First," I asked myself, 'We always see zombies eating brains and guts, but we never see any change after they eat. What does that nourishment do for them? Why can't they be more than mindless eating machines?' From there, I just incorporated the ideas of love and family loyalty.

Shred
Brian Pedersen

Brian Pedersen, 33, currently works as a high school English teacher and previously worked in the field of journalism for several years. He also works as a freelancing writer for an engineering company, focusing on current technology topics. In his spare time, he writes short stories and is working on completing two novels. He has had several short stories published since he started to submit work in 1999. He has had short fiction appear in the print publications Cthulhu Sex, Dark Notes from New Jersey, Tales from a Darker State, Black Petals, Burning Sky, *and online at* horrorfind.com. *Brian currently serves as the vice president of the Garden State Horror Writers. Formerly a New Jersey resident, he now lives in Easton, PA with his fiancé Peggy and their two cats.*

"*L*et's hurry up, we're going to miss *House*! You know it's my favorite show."

Sarah grabbed his hand and pulled him along. Jake stopped walking and refused to budge.

She stopped pulling him and he heard her soft gasp. Without turning away, he realized she was looking at the same thing. The sight of the man on the rooftop reminded Jake of the sniper he once saw on his first assignment.

He and Sarah both stared up at the man in the suit standing motionless on the highest point of the roof of the house, briefcase clutched in one hand, wispy tufts of hair billowing in the bitter February wind.

He appeared to be staring back at them, as if daring them to move. Jake felt his scalp tighten as the old fear of the sniper returned. He had been so vulnerable, out in the open and willing to risk his life for the story. He had to get the story then, and even now, several years later, the journalist within him began to stir. Jake thought it odd, here was a man, about middle-aged, in a three-piece suit getting ready to either survey the property or jump off the roof. What was he doing up there?

His overactive imagination ran away with him. This had to be some guy who simply lost it watching too many episodes of *American Idol*, his brain rotting away behind the blue glow of the TV. Jake felt convinced that TV was doing something horrible to people. He just couldn't convince his girlfriend, or just about anyone else of that. The man couldn't be dangerous, but Jake's reporter instincts told him otherwise. *Fuck this guy. I want the story*, thought Jake. *Who did he think he was, some kind of nut? He's mine. Right here in my hometown of P'burg, a wonderfully nutty little story was sprouting while me and my girl are out for a*

Sunday stroll. The boys at the paper would never believe it. It landed right in my lap.

"Would ya look at that?" Jake whispered. He took out the little spiral notebook he always carried around with him in his back pocket and began jotting down details. He looked over at Sarah, who chuckled.

"C'mon, this guy freaks me out," she said, leaning closer to him so he could smell her peppermint Orbit gum. "Why don't we just leave him alone?"

He squeezed her hand and gave her a quick kiss on the neck. "We will, I really just wanna see what I can find out first."

He hated the look of disappointment that shone in her eyes, knowing it would harden into sadness before flaring into anger. She always did hate those late night sessions he pulled at the paper and the ability he had to tune out all else, including her, when fixated on a story. The rift between them had gotten smaller, but now it moved back to familiar territory. It didn't take long. She glared at him with smoldering eyes and Jake knew he could have easily have gotten moving, but he ignored her fiery stare.

"I just need my camera. Would you mind getting it?" he said, his heart pounding in his head.

She shot him a disapproving look and turned away from the roof. Jake looked back up at the man, only to see him tremble and fall out of sight.

"Holy shit!" Jake shouted, his eyes scanning the roof.

"What?" she said softly, a touch of fear in her voice. She reached for his hand again, her long wispy hair picked up by the steady wind.

Again, he refused to budge.

"C'mon Jake. I wanna go inside. It's getting cold. I don't see him there any more."

"That's because he just fell," he said, staring at the spot where the man stood just seconds ago. Jake whipped out his cell phone and called 9-1-1. He talked to the operator and explained the situation. The moment felt surreal. All the time, he felt Sarah's eyes on him, haunted, puzzled.

"Oh my God," she whispered.

He ran to the house and around to the backyard, finding no one. He knocked on the door and pounded on the windows, calling out. *Why would a home inspector be on a roof, in February. In a suit? Why did he just fall down? I wonder if he's okay? It just didn't make any sense.* Having just moved to the neighborhood, he wasn't familiar with the people, and he was a good four blocks from his house, on a one-way side street off Route 22. He began to take down any details he could. The reporter in him began to take over. He thought back to the time he captured the sniper live, on video. Those were the big city days. He was the envy of the newsroom once. Now he was relegated to small town newspaper status. All those cutbacks and that lousy pay. He often wondered if it was even worth it and yet, once the reporter bug bit him, he found it difficult to ignore it.

He looked back at Sarah, who stared at him with a mixture of shock and anxiety. He took several steps towards the house and stopped.

"Jake!" she called. "Don't go near there! They'll be here any minute. Let them handle it." As soon as she spoke the words, he heard the wail of sirens in the distance.

*

Sarah stayed with him for several more moments before turning and going back towards home. Jake had barely noticed.

He was too busy taking notes and interviewing some of the neighbors who gathered around to gawk, even though he and Sarah appeared to be the only witnesses. He didn't have his press pass with him, so he couldn't get into the house, and nobody would talk to him or give him an official quote, but he found out through the neighbors that the guy had been found on the roof. He had almost slid off, but had been lying prostrate on the roof, part of his hand hanging off the edge in one of the corners, a spray of blood around his head. He had no wallet, no identity.

The cops had even talked to Jake, since he was the sole witness to the man's death. Unfortunately, he didn't have much to add.

*

"It shreds your brain. It just takes you right out."

"What does?" the woman asked. She crossed and then uncrossed her legs again. She was no Sharon Stone, but she wasn't half bad, Jake thought.

He wanted to flip the channel, but was curious as to what the woman was talking about. As he lay in the darkness, his mind still tried to wrap around the strange sight of the man on the roof earlier today. The local TV news station had done a brief report of the incident and he watched the same report on several channels. Then it was back to this odd talk show. Jake looked over at Sarah, the TV casting a blue glow over her sleeping face. "This madness. It gets inside your skull and when it gets to be too much, it just rips itself out," the woman continued. "Once it gets in, there's no way out."

Jake still didn't know what she meant, and he was just about to turn it off when he felt Sarah tighten her grip on his hand. A soft gasp escaped her throat. Jake looked at her more closely.

Probably just having a nightmare, he thought.

"But where is it coming from?" asked another woman who was off camera. "This thing, what do you call it? Shred? Where did it start? This all seems so unreal."

Sarah loosened her grip.

To Jake it felt unreal and frustrating all at the same time, and it was giving him a headache. *Who was this woman? What was she talking about?* The thing he hated about TV is you often turned it on and you were stuck in the middle of things, not knowing what the hell was going on. He hated TV so much that he never had one until he started living with Sarah. He remembered only vaguely watching it when he was a teenager living at home. *Newspapers are where it's a*t. That's where he got all his news from, but unfortunately, it was a dying art. No one wanted to read anymore, not with TV and now the Internet.

Jake mused about the man on the roof. He thought about his own youthful compulsion to climb high places. It didn't matter where they were. When he was a teenager, he and his friends would sneak up to the roofs of office buildings, supermarkets, just about anywhere, even though Jake was secretly afraid of heights. He always had a phobia of falling, but in many ways, he enjoyed the thrill of climbing high places, at least then. He certainly wouldn't want to try it now. Maybe the man was simply bored and wanted to do something dangerous.

Sarah woke up and smiled at him, giving him a deep kiss. He hugged her and squeezed her, his hands finding her smooth bare skin. "I love you," she whispered, staring deeply into his eyes. He repeated it back to her; grateful that for the first time in his life, he was with someone with whom he really meant it. He slid his hand down across her smooth stomach down under the thin fabric of her panties.

She frowned and reached for the remote control and changed the channel to one of her favorite reality TV shows. He felt a twinge of anger flare up within him. He sighed and got up off the bed. *He thought again about what the woman on TV said. What did she call it? Shred. That's it. Some type of disease that makes your brain explode? Of course the woman was crazy. But why was it something that sounded like it could happen?*

He went into the study in the next room and began to look through his books. He tried to find something interesting to read, even though most of the stuff he'd read already. He found a tattered copy of *The Shining* by Stephen King, one of his old faves.

He heard a strange noise right outside the window. It almost sounded like something heavy hitting the ground. He peered out between the slats on the mini blinds but saw nothing. He grabbed his notebook and jotted some more thoughts down. The story continued to work on him, but he found little to do with it. He needed some sources. After several moments of staring at the scribbled notes, he sank into his favorite chair with his book, which was something that always made him relax. He glanced up at the recent photos that dotted the mantel around his fireplace. He liked being surrounded by pictures of his earlier days. Here he was at his 30th birthday bash. The guys had taken him out to a strip club and then bar hopping. There he was winning the award for the sniper story, his first piece several years ago. His hair began to stand on end as he remembered each excruciating detail. Never had he felt so alive in that moment when the cops nabbed the guy and he had gotten a close up and an exclusive interview with one of the captives.

There he was with Sarah. One of the first photos they had taken together. This one was by a brook and it was so spontaneous, the two of them, laughing like those who are still in the early throes of love, testing each other out and succumbing to the glorious thrills. Sunlight danced on their faces. Sarah was hugging him and laughing uncontrollably. Sometimes the happiest moments that he could think of were when he made her laugh. It just made him feel real good inside.

"Sarah?" He called out into the darkness. "Sarah, are you awake?"

Only the sound of her soft breathing and gentle snoring met him, along with the voices from the TV. He sighed, got up and walked out of the room and over to his side of the bed, careful not to smack his shins into the chest at the foot of the bed. He turned the TV off.

He slid in next to her and lay on his back, listening to the sound of her sleeping. Finally, at some point in the night, it lulled him into his own slumber.

He awoke to the sound of her heavy breathing. She twisted and turned next to him, her face a grimace of unease and terror. She had to be having another nightmare. The blankets were violently yanked from him and he was left with a feeling of coldness. She turned over on her side and then she was silent. Her breathing grew calm and less restless. Finally, her breathing returned to normal and he heard the soft, faint hum of the train in the distance. It was a sound that had always comforted him as a child, but now it filled him with a horrible sense of impending dread.

He reached over to Sarah and held her clenched hand.

He squeezed it and tried to slow his ragged breathing. For several moments, nothing moved, no sound issued forth. Then he heard a high-pitched wheezing and turned to face her. Her face moved frantically back and forth, as if she were involved in a seizure and her mouth contorted into a grimace.

She screamed out and clutched him. Her eyes opened and regarded his with a look of contempt. He was filled with fear and a sense of foreboding. He couldn't imagine what was happening. He thought back to the man on the roof.

He held her and tried to shake her out of her stupor. Then he got out of bed and flicked the light on. He cried out her name but she still didn't answer him. Then, just as quickly as the episode overtook her, she lay still.

Her mouth closed and she breathed in and out softly, as if in a deep sleep.

He slowly relaxed and let his mind slip away. He flicked the light off and got back in bed. Surprisingly, he found himself drifting away, falling asleep and following where his mind went into a silky, leaden slumber.

The next morning he awoke and his mind felt dull, listless. He heard the voices on the TV again. He remembered turning it off last night. She must have turned the TV on at some point in the night. He got out of bed, opened the blinds and stared at the day, which was bathed in a glow of white from the early morning snow.

He turned around and looked back at Sarah where she lay sleeping soundlessly on the bed. He sat on the bed and watched her. Her breathing grew more rapidly. He turned off the TV and listened to her. He felt the sudden need to open a window. He got up and walked over to it, pressing his fingers against the cool pane. He pushed it open and let the smooth air in. It felt refreshingly warm for a moment, and he imagined that spring would be around the corner even though it was months away. Outside, two children played in a patch of soft, muddy snow, their voices carrying swiftly through the open window.

He looked back at her sleeping form, thinking the breezy noise would wake her. He gently touched her naked body through the sheets. Still, she didn't move. He decided he would surprise her and make her breakfast. Her favorite thing to eat was scrambled eggs and toast, with a mug of fresh brewed coffee with milk. He trotted downstairs and began getting things ready. As he was beating the eggs, he heard the creak and groan of the bed above him, and her soft footsteps treading through the bedroom.

He was glad to see that she had gotten up. *Maybe some food and coffee would make her feel better.* Plus, there was the added bonus of his decision to surprise her, which could only have added benefits for him. He thought about her snug, sleeping form and how good she would feel. He had ordered her a bouquet of fresh flowers and knew they were supposed to be delivered today. He couldn't wait to surprise her with them. He knew they would brighten her mood.

He finished cooking, put the oven on the preheat setting, and placed the food on plates and closed the oven to keep the breakfast warm for a few minutes. He decided to put on some music to get him going and was surprised to find a news station. He usually always had it set to the local rock station.

"You mean there's people falling off of roofs?" It was a man's voice, gruff and deep. "How could this be? You're saying people are willingly climbing up onto roofs and deliberately falling off of them? Listen, no listen to me Howard. This makes absolutely no sense. No sense at all." The man laughed then. "You've gotta be kiddin' me."

Jake heard a stirring in the bedroom. "Jake? Jake?" Sarah was calling him.

He concentrated on the loud drone of the news station. "Hold on, I'm listening to something important here."

He didn't like to think about what the man was saying. It all seemed so surreal.

Now another man's voice interrupted the speaker. He had a slightly rougher, older sounding voice. "It must be something with the antennae maybe. Maybe they are just trying to communicate with...oh, I don't know, *something*. Something we just aren't familiar with. I don't know Bill, but I'm telling you, there's something seriously wrong here. It's happening all over and I...

Jake cut him off and turned the station, but he caught more snatches of the same thing, happening all over. He remembered he left his cell phone in the car and had to recharge it before he went out today. He tried to tell himself to stay calm. He grabbed his keys and ran outside to his car, which was parked in the driveway. He got the cell phone and turned around. When he looked back up at the house he gasped in terror.

Dressed in only a thin nightgown, Sarah stood on the roof, at the highest point of the house. Already her legs wobbled and trembled, struggling to hold up her slim weight. For several seconds, Jake was completely paralyzed and unable to move. Then he sprinted for the house, calling her name as he leapt inside and climbed up the stairs.

He dialed 9-1-1 as he ran through the bedroom and to the open window, remembering what the woman on TV said. What he couldn't bear to think about.

"Shred. It happens to all of us. Sooner or later."

He pushed the window open more and climbed out, pressing away his phobia of falling. He stared down at the smooth pavement of the driveway, cursing his fear as it tried to overtake him. He pushed it away and focused instead on Sarah. On his sweet Sarah and her muffled, anguished cries, the scraping of her feet against the tiles of the roof, her heavy, labored breathing.

The wind picked up and pushed him on as she stumbled along the peak.

"Sarah!" He cried. "Hold on! I'm coming!"

His fingers struggled to gain a hold on the ragged tiles, which were dotted with snow. The early morning sun had already warmed them and the cold air steadily grew warmer.

"Sarah, here." He held out his hand. "Take it."

She refused to budge, and her eyes grew distant and vacant.

She held her hands to her head and grimaced, closing her eyes.

He stared at her fingers, which were bloody from scratching and clawing at the roof.

She cried out in pain. "I can feel it inside my head. Tearing everything away." She let out a cry of anguish that shocked him to the core.

He looked around, and was astonished to see that on the roofs of other houses all around their neighborhood, as far as he could see, other people were falling off, one by one.

Bethany, an older woman who was their next-door neighbor, spasmed and fell backwards. Her neck snapped like a twig as it hit the corner of her roof and a burst of blood sprayed the siding. Earl and Brenda, a couple who were close to Jake and Sarah's age were on the next roof over, and when Brenda hit the edge of the roof her neck snapped back.

"Oh my God Sarah! We have to get down from here! C'mon!"

He grabbed her then, and tried pulling her down, but she refused, her arms surprisingly strong. He pulled harder but fell backwards, sliding down the side of the roof. All around him, he heard anguished sighs, followed by groans, thuds, and startled cries as bodies fell to the ground. He slid over the edge and grasped onto the gutter. He felt the creaking and bending and heard the groan as the gutter slowly gave way.

He caught a final glimpse of Sarah as she fell backwards, out of sight, her eyes filled with anguish.

He felt the snap of the gutter as his fingers became free and then just had time to utter a cry of agony before the ground met his bones, silencing all sensation.

What inspired "Shred"?

I recently moved to Easton, PA and decided to set this story in Philipsburg, New Jersey, the next town over the river. I got the idea for Shred after taking a walk through the neighborhood during a cold, January day with my girlfriend, Peggy. On one of the streets, we came across this man standing on the roof of a house in what looked like a long trenchcoat. It looked as though he was holding a briefcase and I felt like he was staring at us. The image stuck in my head because it just didn't gel. I knew I had to build a story and some characters around it. We never did find out what he was doing up there. We just kept walking.

Temperature Days on Hawthorne Street

Charles Grant

Dark fantasy writer/editor Charles Grant was born in 1942 and received his B.A. in History/English from Trinity College (Connecticut) in 1964. He then taught English, history, and drama in high schools before being drafted into the army (VietNam). He served eight years as an officer of the Science Fiction Writers of America, ten years on the Board of Directors of the World Fantasy Awards, was past president of the Horror Writers of America, served five years as President of the Board of Trustees of HWA, and was on the board of advisors for The Burry Man's Writers Center. In 1987 he received the British Fantasy Society's Special Award, for life achievement. In May 2000, he received the Lifetime Achievement Award from HWA. In addition, he has received two Nebula Awards and three World Fantasy Awards for his writing and editing. He is most remembered, though, for his quiet horror (The Pet, Something Stirs, Raven, Stunts, Jackals, the Millennium Quartet, and many others, including the Oxrun Station books) and for his landmark anthology series, Shadows. He was married to editor/novelist Kathryn Ptacek for nearly 25 years. Charlie died on September 15, 2006, three days after his birthday.

*T*he half-moon porch was partially masked by untrimmed arms of fully green forsythia and juniper dying at the tips. What breeze there was in pressing heat only caused to quaver the languid drone of hunting bees. A spider, working steadily in the shaded corner of a peeling post and sloping roof, ambushed a fly while a mantis lurking on the lattice flanking the steps watched, praying. There were ants, marching, but the man on the bottom step ignored their parade, waiting instead for the sounds of anger to drain from the house. He rubbed his face, tugged at his chin, blaming the summer-long heat for the pots he heard slamming onto the stove, the crack of cabinet doors, the thud and hollow roll of an empty can on the linoleum floor. He hunched at the sharp noises and glanced up the block, wondering why none of the houses to the top of the gentle hill had emptied at the aftermath of the fight.

Sounds carried on a street like this, he thought, like the night the week before when Casper Waters had ordered his wife to pack and leave just before the late evening news. By the time she had limped with a suitcase to her car and had driven around the corner, not a porch was deserted, not a lawn with flickering flashlights carried by men ostensibly searching for lost tools. So now where are they, he wondered at the blank facades of Hawthorne Street. They're no better than I am. Why the hell don't they come out?

The milkman, he answered himself. They've figured the bogeyman milkman has done it again, and some of them believe it, and they're as afraid as I am.

A robin landed silently beneath one of the front yard's two ancient willows and cocked a brown eye toward the lawn.

"Gerry?"

It pecked twice and fluttered, hopping rapidly across the slate walk to the other side, where it pecked twice again and flew off.

"Gerry?"

He leaned backward, feeling the ragged edge of the step pressing against his spine, and tilted his head until his neck stretched close to choking. Ruth, her night-soft hair twisted back to a ponytail and wisping around her temples, looked down at him, trying to manipulate muscles that once made her smile. One softly tanned hand lay flat against her stomach, and he suddenly wished the baby would hurry up and show itself; his first daughter had kept Ruth slim, and had died before birth. He closed his eyes briefly, then stretched up a palm, holding it open until she covered it and came down beside him.

"They must be tired of men beating their wives," he said quietly, waving his free hand toward the street. "Not even old lady Greene's left her precious garden."

Nearly four years ago he would have been a father for the second time.

"Gerry, I'm sorry."

"Don't be silly, lover," he said. "You've nothing to be sorry for. I'm the one who started it. I guess I'm not used to such heat in September."

Smiling then, she rested her cheek against his damp shoulder, and they watched for an hour the shadows of the willows glide away from the house. A lawn mower sputtered; a gaggle of small girls shrieked by in pursuit of a dream; there were birds and clustering gnats, and a Siamese cat that disdained Gerry's enticements for the stalking of a jay. Then, explosive, a trio of boys sped past on bicycles, shouting and gesturing to one another before separating at the block's center, one to swerve widely and thump over the curb, mischievous bravado in the skid that came to a halt inches from the juncture of step and walk.

"Hi," he said, with Ruth's thin lips and Gerry's heavy jaw.

"I'm too young for a heart attack," Gerry said, noticing absently the clotted mud on the boy's jeans. "Put the bike away and wash up. We're going to eat; your mother's tired."

"She asleep?" his son whispered loudly.

"No," Ruth said, keeping her eyes shut. "I'm recovering from shock. One of these days you're going to hit these steps and wind up in pieces all over the porch." It should have been a joke, but the boy knew it wasn't. "Your father," she added, aware of the strained silence. "Your father just painted it last summer."

"It'll never happen," he said, laughing as he walked the bicycle around to the side of the house. "How much time?"

"Not enough time for you to call that girl," Gerry said. "Just wash up and get on out here. And change those pants."

"Maybe the milkman will bring me a new pair. I've sure messed this one up."

Ruth immediately sat up, preparing to stand, when Gerry grabbed her firmly by the wrist. "Relax," he said. "Sandy didn't mean anything by it. He doesn't know for sure. None of the kids do."

A joke, Gerry had thought in a long-ago May when the grass was new and the smell of it cut filled the neighborhood like meadowed incense. In addition to the family's usual order for milk, eggs, and butter, he had added at the bottom of the note a mocking request for a clean shirt when Ruth had forgotten to do one up for him the evening before. They had laughed and gone to bed, and the following morning a package lay beside the milkbox. Inside was a shirt the proper size and perfect color for the suit he had been planning to wear.

"Now this is the kind of milkman I like," he said, but Ruth, though laughing, was uneasy. "Oh, come on, woman," he said. "This guy obviously appreciates a joke. I'll just leave the box if it'll make you feel better, and I'll bet it will be gone the next time he comes. Okay?"

He did, and when the plain-wrapped package remained, he only shrugged and shoved the shirt to the bottom of his dresser drawer. Ruth asked him to get up early enough to give it back personally; she was wary of gifts from a man they'd never seen.

"Now you're being silly," he said, more stubbornly than he had intended. "I'll be damned if I'm going to get up before dawn just to give a stupid milkman back his shirt. Besides, it's a pretty nice one, you said so yourself. I'll just wait for the bill and see how much he nails me for it."

There was a week before the payment notice arrived, itemizing nothing more than the dairy products they'd consumed. Gerry shrugged again and decided the shirt was a present. He assumed it was a clever bit of maneuvering for a whopping Christmas gift but did not mind since he had planned after the first delivery to do it anyway. The Sweet Milk Dairy Farm was a firm he'd never heard of and decided was an independent farmer. Since he was willing to patronize the little guy over the big guy, especially one whose service provided unexpected benefits and the best-tasting buttermilk he'd had since he was a kid, he ignored Ruth's misgivings.

Shortly afterward, he needled Ruth into asking for something, and when she proved as intransigent in her refusals as he was in his insistence, he petulantly added a request for a tie to match the shirt. And when it came, in a plain-wrapped box, he laughed all day, shaking his head and telling his friends at the office what a tailor he had. Bolder then, he decided to ask for a suit to go with the shirt and tie; and this time, when the hand-tailored-to-fit-no-one-else sharkskin garment hung on a nail over the mailbox, he stopped laughing and began wondering what kind of racket he was getting himself into. Ruth, he noticed with some relief, had not said a word but placed the suit at the back of the closet, still wrapped in its clear plastic bag.

"You got to admit," he said at dinner one evening when Fritz Foster and the Yorks had joined them, "the man's a go-getter. I just wish he'd send me a bill or something. Ruth here thinks he might be peddling stolen goods. I've been thinking about asking around the police myself, to tell the truth."

Syd York, puff-cheeked and portly, glanced at his wife, who nodded, and Gerry's eyebrows raised in question. "Yeah, yeah," Syd admitted. "We've been picking up a few things here and there ourselves. Like you, we figured it was some kind of joke but ... what the hell, right? I don't ask questions, and I get what I want. There was a set of golf clubs, a pair of shoes and ... what else, dear?"

Aggie, her husband's twin, pointed at her mouth with her fork apologetically. Syd snapped his fingers. "Of course, how could I forget. Silverware! Aggie was complaining about the stuff we use in the kitchen, and when I got my clubs, she snuck in a note for the knives and forks. Damn, but didn't we get real silver."

Aggie grinned, and Ruth only stared at her coffee.

Fritz placed his utensils on his empty plate and leaned back, his fingers tucking inside of his belt. "I asked for money."

The women looked at him. Syd laughed, and Gerry only shook his head, not surprised that the block's resident investment broker would be the one to get practical with their dawn genie.

"How much?" he asked. "That is, if you don't mind me getting personal."

"Let's just say substantial, and I received every dime."

"Well, didn't you ask him where he got it?"

Fritz grinned at Ruth and shook his head. "I don't ask, my dear, I just take. The money was in large bills, and when I took it to the bank, it was good. As long as I don't see his face in the post office, what do I care how he operates, as long as he keeps up the good work."

"Besides," Syd added, "how could you know him? None of us have ever seen him."

It had been like moving into another country, Gerry recalled thinking when he and Ruth deserted the city and the routine of the neighborhood settled over them like a worn and welcome sweater. The mailman knocked at every door and knew all the streets by name; a policeman walked the beat three times daily and was covered by a patrol car whose brace of blue was as familiar as the century-old maple on the corner. Through traffic was negligible, and the street was covered with markings for baseball and hopscotch and spur-of-the-moment games comprehensible only to the young. And the milkman, who might have used a fly-bitten horse for all the inhabitants knew, passed each dawn, and only the early-risers and insomniacs heard the clatter of empty bottles as he left each back door more silent than shadow.

No one tried to wake early enough to see him; an unspoken warning about breaking their charm.

As June released summer, children, and, sporadically, husbands, Gerry thought he noticed increasing reluctance to try their luck again. Indeed, they all seemed rather guilty about suspecting their good fortune and began ordering more dairy products than most of them could use. Then Syd, after drinking himself into melancholy on Gerry's porch, asked for a raise, and two days later he was promoted.

"Now that was definitely a coincidence," Gerry said. "I can understand a guy trying to pick up an extra buck peddling goods from God knows where, but there's no way a stupid milkman can get a guy a raise like that."

Ruth immediately agreed, but her face was drawn, and he didn't learn until it was too late that she had finally contributed her own request. It was a Saturday morning when he backfired into the driveway and saw the sleek and gleaming automobile parked in front of the house. In the kitchen, Ruth was crying at the table. Confused, since there didn't seem to be any company in the house, he cradled her softly while she explained that she could no longer stand the daily wait for the call from the police saying he and their twelve-year-old car had died in the traffic.

"I thought about Syd, Gerry, and I was scared, but I put a note in, and this morning this man comes up with a receipt saying we won this car, and we have to pay the taxes but we have a week from this Monday, and I wish it was gone because I'm frightened."

Ridiculous, Gerry thought, coincidence. But nevertheless, he went to bed early and set the alarm for an hour before dawn, thinking the hell with the charm if it was going to do this to his wife.

In not entirely unpleasant contrast to the daylight's enervating heat, the morning was cold, and a residue wind from an evening thunderstorm hunted through the neighborhood for wood to creak and leaves to sail. Silently dressing in the clothes he'd left in the kitchen, Gerry sipped on hot coffee and rubbed his arms briskly. A groan from Sandy's sleep made him motionless, then he slipped a blanket over his shoulders and carefully opened the front door, picking out a chair on the far end of the porch where he could watch the walk that wound round the house to the back. He lighted a cigarette when he was settled, and he was startled by the flare of the match and shook it out quickly. He listened and heard nothing, watched and saw only the dark. The air was still damp, and he hugged himself tightly but would not walk, knowing the floorboards made near as much noise as the children playing in the afternoon. Finally, he tried to count gorillas to pass the time, and when he awakened, the sun was full in his eyes, and blinding.

Ruth was standing over him, smiling sadly. "Big brave watchdog," she said, offering him a steaming cup. "What were you going to do, sprinkle garlic over his horns or tackle him like the football star you thought you were?"

"Knock it off," Gerry said, feeling bad enough that his soap opera plan had failed without his wife telling him how foolish he looked wrapped in a blanket in the middle of August. "Did he leave anything?"

"Nothing."

"Well, damnit, he must have magicked me to sleep, or something. And I asked for a hundred dollars."

"Maybe he figures you were testing him," she said, leaning against the railing and huddling her arms under her breasts. "Maybe he doesn't like testing."

Gerry, suddenly angry because he was more than afraid, stood abruptly and started pacing. "You know, I should have listened to you, because you were right from the beginning. This guy is up to no good. I think I'll cancel the contract, and we can get our milk from the store from now on." Then he glared because his wife was laughing. "Well, what's so funny, damnit? I spent a miserable time out here, I could have maybe even caught double pneumonia, and you think that's funny?"

Shaking her head, Ruth pressed into his arms and quieted. "No, dear, I don't think it's funny. In fact, I think it's kind of sad. Things are just so different out here, I can't really explain it. The city was bad, but at least we knew where we stood. Here, we get a little boost from an invisible milkman and we go into melodramatic hysterics. Maybe country rules are different, I don't know, but there's something wrong with us."

"What?" Gerry said.

"I'm not sure," she said. "But this isn't right."

A short exclamation from Ruth and a dry flurry dragged him reluctantly back to the present where the world appeared to be turning black at the edges of his vision. Feeling a shudder from Ruth, he looked down and saw a praying mantis disappearing over the side of the steps with what looked like the remains of a spider in its jaws.

*

"Do you want to change before we go out?" he asked quietly, wondering what was taking his son so long. Ruth shook her head slowly, and he was dismayed at the ridges of darkened skin beneath her eyes, cursing himself for not noticing her condition sooner. To adjust from the city's frantic years had been difficult enough when she was the proliferation of little girls Hawthorne Street had spawned, but the addition of the pregnancy in the century's worst summer was draining her of laughter; she had been claiming since the beginning that the baby hadn't felt right, and no amount of persuasion from husband or doctor could change her mind. And if I told her about the milkman, Gerry thought, she might literally kill me. Finally he eased a solicitous arm about her shoulders and drew from her a melancholy smile.

"I spoke with Syd on the golf course this morning," he said after calling for Sandy to get a move on. "We've decided to confront the dairy company—"

"Please, Gerry, I don't want to hear it."

"Oh, come on, Ruth, let's not start again, please? This milkman business is getting all out of hand. I don't see why you're letting it get to you like this. I mean, no one else is all that bothered."

"Well, maybe nobody else cares whether or not they're doing the morally right thing by letting this farce continue the way it has," she said angrily, shrugging away his arm. "I told you before, I don't want that man, beast, whatever the hell he is, coming to my house anymore. Suppose Sandy starts sneaking notes to him? Suppose the other kids find out this isn't a game? Suppose ..." She turned to him, and he flinched at the hardened lines destroying her mouth. "Suppose one of you big brave men gets tired of his wife and asks for a new one? What happens then?" Her hands went protectively across her stomach, accusing him with their barrier, and he realized that she suspected what he had done.

Suddenly angry to camouflage his fear, he paced to the sidewalk and back, his hands fisted in his pockets. "What the hell are you talking about," he demanded as slowly and flatly as he could. "A few ties, a few shirts, one lousy set of golf clubs, and everyone—no, you go flying off the goddamned handle. Tell me, do you see anyone else on this block worried? Do you see the place crumbling in moral decay just because a milkman runs a shoddy little business on the side?"

"What about Syd's promotion and the new car?"

Gerry spun around, frustration at his wife's persistence threatening to erupt in shouting. "Syd has been with that firm for fifteen years, and a promotion was just plain due. I won that bloody car in a raffle at the office, and what the hell more explanation do you want anyway, Ruth?"

"The hundred dollars."

"For crying out loud, I didn't get it."

"Yes," she said. "Yes, you did."

Gerry stopped just as Sandy ran out the front door and flopped next to his mother, grinning. "Well?" he said. "We going or not?"

"In a minute," Gerry said to him before turning back to Ruth. "What are you talking about, Ruth? What hundred dollars?"

Ruth obviously did not want to continue the argument in front of their son, but Gerry's face, in an uncontrollable sneer, forced her to ignore him. "In the mail, while you were out with your precious friends on that precious golf course. A check from the insurance company. Overpayment."

Gerry froze, the sun suddenly chilling as he loosened and began waving his hands impotently in the air. "Nonsense," he said. "Pure nonsense."

"Then what about this baby?" she said, throwing the question like scalding water into his face. She stood then, swaying, crying silently, her head shaking away what answers he might have had. Sandy gaped before reaching up to her, but she only cried out and ran into the house.

"Dad?"

Gerry fumbled in his hip pocket, pulling out his wallet from which he yanked the first bill his fingers could grip. "Here," he said hoarsely, extending the money blindly, "take the bike and grab some hamburgers or something. I ..." He looked helplessly at his son, who nodded and left without a word. When he returned with his bike, Gerry looked at him. "Your sister," he started but could not finish.

"I know, Dad," he said. "Today should have been her birthday, right?"

Gerry nodded mutely and stared as his son wheeled into the street and vanished around the corner; the boy seemed so old. He watched the empty sidewalks until his legs began to tremble; then he shuffled to the porch and sought out his chair in the far corner, remembering the night he had waited and slept, and the morning when Ruth had smiled and laughed at him. Though he didn't see how it was possible, he was positive Ruth knew he had asked the milkman for a daughter to replace a daughter. He had done it, he told himself every evening in freeflowing nightmares, because she needed it, because the two of them had been too afraid to try again only to renew the pain.

"Insane," he muttered to a hovering bee.

And did she know, he wondered, that Casper Waters had asked for his freedom and had found his wife naked in bed with Fritz Foster?

"Insane."

"I'll tell you," Syd had whispered confidentially at the course that morning, "If I had the nerve, I'd dump Aggie in a minute for a twenty-year-old girl without ten tons of fat."

Perversely, the temperature climbed as the sun fell, and perspiration on his neck trickled warmly to his chest and back. Cicadas passed him a childhood warning of the next day's heat, and he dozed, fitfully, swiping flies in his sleep, flicking a spider from his shoulder. Up the street there was music, and Sandy drifted back for permission to accept a last-minute invitation to a block party over the hill. Inside, the house was dark though he had heard Ruth stumble once in the living room.

Embryos floating through ink and white blood, their faces not his, not hers, blank and unfilled and waiting for a wish from unarmed despair.

There was a rattling far back in his dreams that twisted his head until he snapped awake and heard the footsteps on the walk.

"Hey," he said sleepily, and the footsteps halted. "I, uh, was just kidding about the daughter bit, you know." He shook his head but remained groggy and nodding, his speech slurred though he heard himself clearly. "I mean, let's face it, shirts are one thing, a kid's another, you know what I mean? Hey, you know what I mean?"

There was a silence before the clinking resumed and Gerry slept on, dreaming pink and white lace, until he awakened, the sun barely rising, to Sandy's shouts for help and Ruth's hysterical screaming.

The story adapted...

Charles Grant's story was adapted for television's Tales from the Dark Side, for an episode entitled "The Milkman Cometh." His work has inspired a generation of writers who recognize Grant as a true master of quiet, subtle horror.

Sucker Kiss
Edward Greaves

Edward Greaves was born in 1970 in a blue collar Bergen County town. It might have been his grandfather's tales of old Eire that started his fascination with the fantastic. He soon took to devouring entire sections of the town public library; first fantasy, myth and legend, then branched out into science fiction, mystery and horror. When the library ran out of books, he started crafting his own stories. He attended Rutgers University, where after a tryst with engineering and science, he focused instead on literature, history, and creative writing. Graduating in 1992 with a BA in English, he ended up working in the IT field during the boom years of the internet explosion. He still resides in New Jersey, with his wife—also a life-long New Jersey resident—their new son, and a mop with four legs named after Charlemagne's father.

"**S**orry I'm late." Peter closed the conference room door. "An imp was stuck in a desk and needed extraction." He took the nearest empty seat at the table. Peter leaned over, and his clockwork familiar—a jumble of gears, pins, levers and prongs—slid onto the table with all the quiet of a toolbox being upended.

When the noise subsided, his boss Mark spoke. "I guess *now* we can make our introductions?"

Peter winced. He'd hear about it later for being late again. But when the woman in accounting who makes sure your purchase orders get through without a glitch calls you in a panic over a screaming daemonlet literally embedded in her desktop its head poking out of her keyboard, you don't ignore her.

"I'm Mark Greenberg," said the tall thin man with glasses and curly brown hair. "Director of Wizardry."

Next to him was an older man, more scalp than thin tufts of white hair. "Hello, I'm Gene Lowenbach, Manager of Prognostications."

"I'm Mayur Gupta," said the middle-aged chubby Indian man. "I work for Gene in Prognostications." An understatement—Mayur *was* Gene's team, and did ninety percent of the work.

Peter straightened up as he realized all eyes were on him. "Uh, Peter Walden, Daemonic Contact and Command Systems." Which was a convoluted way to say that he consorted with Daemons, and kept them under control.

Across the table sat a familiar face, Roger their account manager from Hoary Eye Incorporated. "Hello everyone, I believe we've all met. Roger Davies, with Hoary Eye. With me today are Calvin Fields," he nodded to the grey haired black man on his right. "Cal is our product specialist and will be presenting for you today. And Didi Reynolds, your new North Jersey area sales rep."

Roger indicated the forty-something blonde in a navy pant suit, her curly hair cut short. She didn't have model looks, but she was attractive. When she looked at Peter, her smile felt like a wink. She slid a business card across the table to each of them. Peter took the card, and his fingers brushed lightly against hers. Though it was only an instant, it felt as if she'd let her hand linger to make that contact. Peter sat a little taller.

"At this point," said Roger, "I'm going to turn over the presentation to Cal, who will bring you up to date on our product offerings."

Calvin stood up, and clicked on the first slide. In his Chicago accent, he launched into the presentation. Peter paid only cursory attention. Prognostication was the least well-understood form of wizardry, even among wizards. Once Peter learned that you couldn't use it to predict the winner of the next Yankees game, he deemed the whole discipline useless. Corporations, on the other hand, thought otherwise. Future trend analysis, detecting general ebbs and flows in the market, predictive profit computations—all stuff that reminded him far too much of economics. Peter hated economics.

While Calvin spoke in excited tones about products that Gene's group would never be able to afford, Peter's mind wandered. He started doodling on his notepad, sketching a design for a circle of petition. Stuck on the same question of which order to place the vital sigils for supplication, domination, and restraint he scratched out the design. Never a good idea to leave a circle you drew unbroken.

He scanned the room. Gene and Mayur listened attentively to the presenter. Mark carried on a low side conversation with Roger. His eye landed on Didi, and stopped. He couldn't place why, but he felt attracted to her, and he normally didn't go for blondes. Every few seconds, he caught a glance from her, and he felt good. Before he knew it, he was balancing his pen on its point, a trick he used in college to impress girls. He was rewarded with another of her smiles when she noticed and he smiled back. Perhaps it still worked.

*

They took a coffee break from the presentation. Peter, first on line, poured himself a cup from one of the white carafes. His co-workers were still questioning Calvin. He reached for a packet of sugar, and a soft hand touched his. The feeling was electric. He looked up into Didi's smile. This time, he was certain she was flirting.

"Sorry, didn't mean to cut the line," she said.

Peter felt as if he had a mouth full of cotton. "S'okay," was all he could manage. Why did he feel like a high school sophomore, asking out a cheerleader? He moved aside, to make room for her.

"How long have you worked here?" she asked.

Peter swallowed, trying to push down that awkward feeling. "About seven years. Eight years before that with Wellson."

She cringed. Wellson was a consulting firm that famously imploded due to bad business practices. Not that Peter had been anywhere near high enough to be affected by the scandal. Still, he was used to the reaction.

"How did you end up here?" she sipped her coffee.

"Headhunter," he replied. He meant that literally.

He'd come in as a consultant to deal with a daemon that had taken the heads of three employees when it escaped from a summoning gone awry. Most days, he would relate the tale, but it felt like bragging, and he was afraid bragging might be a turnoff.

"You enjoy it here?"

He shrugged. "Always something interesting going on."

She smiled and nodded. Just as she turned to leave, she winked. Or had he imagined that? He watched her walk away. His eyes drifting to her rear before he felt self conscious. She stopped, and laid a hand on Mark's shoulder, leaning over to speak into his ear.

A touch of jealousy welled up, as Peter watched. As he wondered what she said, he caught the look on Calvin's face. Grim anger, as he too watched her interaction with Mark. Somewhere in the back of his brain, Peter felt something amiss.

She moved on, talking next with Mayur, then Gene. Each time, she made some kind of contact. Innocent though the contacts appeared, Peter's body reacted as if Didi was his girlfriend flirting with every man at a party. He eyed the others with mistrust. Mayur was eyeing Calvin suspiciously, even as the other still stared daggers at Mark.

It took effort to turn around, to put his back to everyone else. For several seconds after, images of her not altogether wholesome flashed through his mind; only a determined will kept him from looking back. All he wanted was to catch sight of her again. Instead he stared into his coffee and watched the little whirlpool he made with the stirrer. Ten seconds, twenty, and the urge passed. He took a long sip, then headed out the door.

*

Peter splashed cool water on his face, and stared into the large mirror. He loosened his tie, and unbuttoned his collar. Pulling back the edge of his shirt, he looked at the tattoo below his left collarbone. The pattern remained black. She wasn't using a spell, charm or enchantment. Any direct act of magic would have caused his tattoo to change color.

Could he be overreacting? Maybe she was just a sexy woman, who knew how to flirt well. Or maybe flirting came so naturally, she wasn't aware of it? Perhaps she actually liked Peter and he was imagining the rest because he liked her. Liked her? He'd just met her. They had spoken maybe a dozen sentences. Peter wasn't the type to fawn over someone he just met. There had to be some other explanation.

Peter yanked a towel out of the dispenser, and dried his hands and face. He straightened his shirt and tie in the mirror. He was determined to figure this out.

*

Peter strode into the conference room. Everyone else was seated and ready to go. Even his familiar, sitting idly on the edge of the table, spun its head to watch him enter.

"Sorry. Alex caught me in the hall, and had a few questions," he lied.

Mark nodded, then turned back to his conversation with Didi. In his absence she had changed seats—now she occupied the focal point of the room opposite the screen. Seeing her again, Peter felt self-conscious. Had his suspicion been nothing more than paranoia? How could there be anything wrong with such an innocuous woman. He sat down. Calvin, seeming reluctant, got up to speak again.

He flipped open his PDA, on which he stored the contents of a standard grimoire, the corporate bestiary and series of articles from *Wizardry Now*. He wished for his Spectacles, but the multi-lensed device for examining forces at work were on his desk. He'd have to make do with the few tools he had on hand.

He pulled out the Planerium his Uncle Ferdinand had passed on to him when he'd retired. To most people, it looked like an oversized pocket watch. While it did tell the time, it also gave him critical other information. The current alignment of the planets, the zodiac, the phase and position of the moon—and most importantly, the state of the planes, ethereal, astral, and beyond. The privacy wards weren't active, so the readings should be normal. A examination told him that something was wrong in the ethereal. He snapped shut his Planerium.

"Are you late for something Mr. Walden?" Mark asked. Mark looked paler than his normal pasty self.

"Uh, no." said Peter. "I thought it had stopped, but its fine."

Ethereal meant spirit or daemon. A daemon more powerful than an imp would have difficulty working its power here. The building was well protected from interference of daemonic forces. She could have brought a focus with her into the building, that would bypass some of the defenses. But that's why visitors were scanned by security.

So it wasn't a daemonic power, and his tattoo had already ruled out human magic; that left a spirit. A spirit should have been stopped at the threshold to the building. The only ways he could think of for a spirit to get by were a summoning, or a possession. It had to be a possession. What kind of spirit? He flicked on his PDA, and started searching through the bestiary. The section on spirits was enormous. His specialty was working with daemons, not spirits; making his way through this list was going to take time. Thankfully, with Calvin back in the swing of his presentation, he had time.

Ten minutes of skimming entries told him that he would never find it this way. Not unless he stumbled across the entry by dumb luck. Under other circumstances, he would contact a daemon to search out the information for him. But this was hardly the time or place to summon a daemon. For the first time in years, he had a use for that company issued imp. Too bad it was trapped in a circle in the bottom drawer of his desk. It was an ugly bastard anyway.

The only alternative he had was to contact someone with expertise in spirits and he knew just who. Fumbling with the PDA, he went looking for the text messaging application the IT guys had shown him. Unable to remember which program, he just launched one after another, until he found it. There were twenty-three unread messages for him. He winced—some of them were months old.

He ignored them, and started a new session. He typed awkwardly with his thumbs on the tiny keypad.

>Karen, you there?

There was a long pause.

>Is that Peter? Using technology? I might faint.

She was the type always with the latest—technology or magic made no difference to her.

>Yes. No time. I need help.

Unused to the keypad, he kept his responses brief.

>What's up?

>Spirit. In room. Need to ID.

>Where are you? What's going on?

>Conference Room 240. I think possession.

>Someone's possessed? What's it doing?

>Making people like her.

>That's it?
>LIKE her.
>As in do anything she said? Compulsion?
>No. Like date her. Maybe fight over her.
>Obsessing over her? Want to kiss her?
He paused. It was awkward to admit, but true.
>Yes.
>Did she touch you?
The thought of her touch raised goose bumps.
>Yes.
>Don't. Definitely don't kiss her. Succubus.
>What? Dream?
>Normally they come to men in dreams. Sometimes they can possess a woman. As long as it has her, it can use her to feed on men. Do NOT touch her; she will drain your soul.

He scanned the room. Gene and Mayur were at least attempting to pay attention to the presentation, despite Calvin's increasing distractedness, and occasional pauses to glare at Roger and Mark. Those two sat close to Didi, who kept managing to touch them gently every so often as she spoke. Peter caught a smile and swore that her eyes were sparkling. Despite the distance between them, it was as if staring in her eyes from only inches away. He very much wanted her to be only inches away. Preferably alone and...

The unit was buzzing in his hand. He glanced at the screen.

>Peter. You there? Hello? Peter. PETER!!!
He sighed. That was close.
>Sorry, distracted.
>I bet. Listen. That thing is dangerous. It can kill you. And it could kill her. You can't let it get away. It knows you now, it can track you down, and attack your dreams. You have to capture it. Or destroy it.

Peter sucked in a breath.

>How?

>Spirit bottle.

>Where?

>There's an empty on my desk. Looks like an old atomizer. Read the entry in the bestiary. You have to draw the spirit out. But it will try to attack you. Be careful.

>Thanks Karen.

>Make sure it's a succubus. If I'm wrong, it could be worse.

>I trust you.

>Trust later. Make sure. I'm here if you need backup.

Great, he thought, thirty miles away in Sussex county.

>Thanks.

>Good luck.

He let out the breath he didn't even realize he'd been holding. Then he looked up the entry, and read everything it had on the Succubus. It took considerable will to keep from looking up at Didi as he read. Simple curiosity and the desire to observe her as a specimen as he read the description was strong. The details started to piece together in his mind, and a plan was born.

When they broke for lunch, Peter dashed off.

*

Peter skidded into the cafeteria. Thankfully, it was during a pause between swarms of hungry employees, only a few people on line. He cut to the front, and leaned over the counter to get the attention of the dark haired woman in the chef's outfit.

"Jacky, I need an egg," he said.

"There are other people ahead of you, Peter."

He dismissed them with a wave.

"This is important. I just need an egg. Quick. Raw."

"You want a raw egg?" she asked.

He looked down the line at the angry faces. "Yes, I don't have much time."

She regarded him for a moment, then leaned over, opened up the small refrigerator next to the grill, and took out an egg. She shook her head and handed it over. "Do I even want to know?"

"Thanks. I'll tell you about it later." He headed out.

"Hey," she called out. "Are you going to pay for that?"

"Put it on Mark's budget," he told her, while backing through the door.

*

The entry said Succubi were obsessed with anything involving reproduction. Testicles would have been better, since they were attracted to males, but he didn't think that Jacky kept Rocky Mountain Oysters in stock; not the type of fare served in a New Jersey corporate cafeteria. An egg would have to do. He paused before the open door. Taking a thin needle, he made a tiny hole in the top of the egg, and slid it inside. Once satisfied, he palmed the egg, and walked in.

The plan was simple: put the egg in plain sight, and keep an eye on it. If Didi was possessed by a succubus, she wouldn't be able to help herself. The needle was a risky proposition. Once it pricked her, the iron in the needle would bind the spirit in place. Because it was steel, not pure iron, it would only hold the succubus for a few minutes. The downside was that it would show his hand. The spirit would know that it had been made. That's when things could get dangerous.

Didi had her back to the door, and was leaning against the table. The men were arrayed around her like orbiting planets. Peter didn't spare a glance. He'd been gone for a few minutes, and no one had even taken the wrapping off the lunch platters. He thought about where to place the egg. His first idea was to put it with the salad, but then he thought someone else might mistake it for a hard boiled egg. He tucked it in the middle of the sandwiches, hoping it would look like garnish.

"No one wants any food?" he asked. He picked up a plate and started helping himself.

He heard Didi's heels step up behind him. She laid a gentle hand on his shoulder, making a show of looking over the fare. Peter cringed, knowing now that what had seemed to be the electricity of flirtation, was in fact a part of his essence being siphoned off by the creature. He couldn't let on yet that he knew, and had to endure a few moments of that all too pleasant touch.

"Sorry, let me make room," he said. He took his plate and went back to where his familiar sat on the conference table. He watched from behind as she took a plate, and helped herself. However, the others crowded in behind her. Whether not wanting to be far from her, or just taking the cue to eat, he couldn't tell. He couldn't see the egg. Ducking left and right, he tried to see through the press of bodies, but stopped when he thought it might draw attention.

He half sat on the table and waited. After a few moments, he picked up piece of his salami and provolone hero and munched on it. No reason to skip the free meal.

When the group thinned, he could see the egg was gone. So far, so good—or bad depending on how you looked at it. He glanced at the plates; no one else appeared to have it. Didi, however, had her back to everyone else, facing the corner of the room. Peter felt his heart race. Had it worked?

As if in answer, Didi let out a high pitched scream. Everyone in the room froze, except Peter, who scooped up his familiar, and ran to her.

Her plate crashed to the ground, a mess of salad and eggshell. She spun, eyes searching. Blood dripped from her mouth. That was all the sign Peter needed.

As he closed the distance, he manipulated his familiar, directing it to change shape. She lunged for him, and he snapped his familiar up and around her arms. It locked in place, trapping her hands like a large pair of manacles. She screeched in rage. Swinging both arms hard, and faster than he anticipated, she sent Peter flying a dozen feet away into a row of chairs.

Peter sprawled out on the floor, dazed.

"Help me," she whimpered. "What's he trying to do?"

While Peter was sorting out the aches and pains, the others started acting.

"Peter, what the hell do you think you're doing?" asked Mark.

Calvin interposed himself between Didi, and Peter's prone form.

"Don't listen to her," said Peter.

"What's wrong with him, Mark?" asked Roger. "Get this thing off her."

"I'll do it," said Gene.

"No, don't!" cried Peter.

Too late, Didi lurched forward, grabbed Gene by the shirt, and pulled him in for a kiss. Gene didn't struggle, he just collapsed in her grasp, and sagged there while she sucked the life out of him. Mark, and Roger stood horrified and Mayur dropped his plate.

Didi dumped Gene's body on the floor, then wiped her mouth with the back of her still shackled hands.

Peter struggled to his feet. Calvin stepped in his path.

"Get out of the way," said Peter, "or I'll go through you."

Calvin put up his fists. "You keep away from her."

"You asked for it," said Peter and took a swing. Calvin ducked out of the way, and jabbed him in the face, hard. Peter stumbled back.

"Calvin! What are you doing?" asked Roger.

"I'm protecting her from this lunatic."

Didi sauntered forward. "Thank you Calvin, there's at least one gentleman here."

"Calvin, it's not Didi you're protecting," said Peter. "There's no time to explain, just get out of my way."

"You keep back."

Peter wasn't sure how much longer the needle would bind the succubus. He reached into his pocket, and palmed the bottle from Karen's desk. He had to place the mouth of the bottle to Didi's mouth. He'd only get one chance—he had to get past Calvin.

Peter rushed him again, this time, to the right, closer to where Didi was standing. Calvin rocked him with a cross that made him stumble, but his momentum carried him beyond...

...into Didi's waiting arms. She grabbed him, and he felt that electric feeling tenfold. This time, instead of a pleasant sexual charge, it was a devouring hunger. And he was the snack. He struggled in her arms, and she smiled.

"Come on Peter," she moaned softly, "just a little kiss."

He could still see blood on her lips. He covered his mouth with his hands, trying to keep her from kissing him. She bit the back of his hand, hard until he moved it. Once he did, she latched on, and kissed. He stopped struggling.

Her eyes went wide, and she tried to pull away, but Peter held on, not letting her break the kiss. The kiss seemed to last forever, as she frantically struggled against it. Then she went limp. Peter kept kissing her. Hands grabbed at his shoulders, but he locked his grip on her head, fingers entwined in her curls, and did not let go.

Her eyes flew open again, and she put up one last panicked thrashing, before sagging in his arms. Peter held her up with one arm, while fishing in his pocket. Out came a tiny silver stopper. He leaned her back, and popped the stopper into his mouth, before laying her gently on the ground.

"Peter...what?" was all Mark managed to get out.

He turned to face an angry Calvin being held back by Roger. Peter opened wide, and took out the tiny bottle, now glowing with a swirling white mist. He coughed.

"Succubus," he said. "She was possessed. It was sucking the life out of us. I think she'll be all right now."

He knelt down, and touched the sequence to make his familiar change back to its normal shape. He felt for a pulse, much harder to find than on the TV shows. After a moment he nodded.

"She's alive. But she'll need to get to a hospital."

Mayur leaned over Gene's corpse, a tear on his face.

Calvin held his hand out to Peter. "Sorry, I didn't realize."

He shook hands. "She got to all of us. Security is part of my job." They didn't know how close an escape they'd had. If he'd missed, or if the bottle had broken during the struggle, they would have all joined Gene.

"Poor Gene," said Peter.

Mark picked up the phone, and called for an ambulance.

"I think that concludes our presentation for today," said Roger.

"I hope so," said Peter, collapsing into a chair. "I'm going to have a ton of paperwork to fill out."

What inspired "Sucker Kiss"?

Choosing to set this story in modern day New Jersey sent me scrounging in my unconscious. It didn't seem like a hard proposal at the time. I mean, I've spent my whole life here. I thought about how I could mix the fantastic with the mundane, instead of a more typical type of fantasy. What could be more mundane than work in a corporate environment? Out came Peter Walden, corporate wizard. It made sense to me, that if magic were real, who else would corner the market on that skill set but Corporate America? That was the start. I sketched out a few ideas, and built up the main character. The story's conflict came to me in that short span of time between when my head hit the pillow and drifting off into dreamland. Sleepy as I was, I made detailed notes on the challenges and secondary characters I needed, some of which were even legible enough the next morning for me to start on the story. I enjoyed working that juxtaposition; the familiarity of the workplace against the elements of a dark magic. It just might make you thankful for a humdrum life in a real office. I mean, when was the last time a demon burst through your cubicle wall and cut the head off the guy sitting next to you? I think if I had to work in Peter's world, I'd ask to telecommute. Wouldn't you?

Excerpts From The Diary of Jared Hafler

Neil Morris

Neil Morris lives in Old Bridge, home of Raceway Park (sorry, Englishtown) and thrash metal capital of the east coast during the mid-80s. Metallica, Anthrax, and the roar of jet cars provided the soundtrack to his formative years — enough to make anyone crazy. He joined the Garden State Horror Writers in 2001, the same year his short story, "White Devil," won the GSHW's Graversen award. Two other stories, "Rolling Red" and "The Last Blowoff," appear in the GSHW anthologies Tales From a Darker State *and* Dark Notes From NJ, *respectively, with the former receiving an honorable mention in the 17th annual* Year's Best Fantasy and Horror *collection. If you should meet him, ask him what the word "gription" means.*

***T**uesday, September 20*
     My name is Jared Hafler and today is my birthday. I am 9 years old. Mom says I am her little man and I should start doing grown up things. She got me this book with Wolverine on the cover and told me I should write something in it every day about my life. I still have to do math and history and spelling and grammar, but Mom says this is more important than all those lessons combined. Mom wants me to write my own story about our family and our fight against Emdo.

Monday, September 26
     Dad went to the town meeting to see Mr. Mahler. He's the mayor of the town I live in and he's the one who wants to take our home. He's been trying to do this since before I was born. He says our farm is a blight which means something ugly or neglected. I knew that definition before I even knew what a dinosaur was. I don't think my home is ugly and Mom and Dad and my twice older brother Jeremy are always busy keeping the trucks working and turning the soil and tending to the Christmas trees. Nobody ever knocks on the door and says our farm is ugly and we should move away. The only one who says that is Mr. Mahler. Dad says it doesn't matter to Mr. Mahler if it's true or not. Blight is just the word rich and powerful people like him use as an excuse to steal the property of hard working Americans like us. Dad alway goes to the meetings because it's his chance to keep telling him so face to face, but he doesn't listen. Mr. Mahler says he will not discuss things out of court. Dad was very angry when he got home. He said Mr. Mahler had him thrown out by two policemen.

Saturday, October 8

Now is when people used to come for pumpkins. Dad tells me there was a time when the lot would be full of cars and there would be so many customers in the field he had to hire extra hands just to keep an eye on them. Towns from all over sent school kids my age on field trips to go pumpkin picking, even our town before the whole Emdo thing began. We don't have any pumpkins this year, mainly because we didn't know if we would be here to harvest them. Dad says he wouldn't want to put all the hard work into growing them and then have them fall into Mr. Mahler's hands. I asked him why he still grows Christmas trees if the same thing can happen to them and he says they're different. He says they're a sign of his faith in God and he will never give them up, even if we're not here or if nobody comes to buy them.

Tuesday, November 1

The cops shined their lights in our windows last night. They park on the side of Matlers Lane and point their spot lights up at the house. I was just falling asleep when my whole room lit up like it was daytime but I knew it wasn't. It was a little scary. The light moved around like it was looking for something, like it was alive or I could feel the person on the other end spying on me. They did it before. Dad always goes out tell them to leave us alone, but they always say they got a report of somebody sneaking around. Dad said they should be ashamed of themselves for bugging us instead of protecting kids on Halloween. Mom cried this morning but then we all went to church tonight and prayed for strength.

Thursday, November 24

Thanksgiving. Not much to be thankful for. It's cold and cloudy and kids with normal homes get to go to New York and see the parade and the balloons. I heard the Spiderman balloon was going to be there. Sometimes I wish I was a superhero like him or Wolverine. I would beat up Mr. Mahler and the cops and anyone else who's mean to us until they're all gone and we get to live on our farm forever. Dad says that's all he wants to do, keep his little corner of the world and pass it on to Jeremy and me if we're willing to take care of it. Dad loves this land, just like grandpa Benjamin did and all the way back to great grandpa Cameron in the olden days. Someone in the family has always looked after this place because it's what they wanted to do. Uncle Mark and aunt Helen are here visiting and they have helped us out a lot, but they moved away and live in Pennsylvania and Maryland. They didn't want the farm. Only Dad did. He's not angry at them for leaving, it's just the way things worked out.

Saturday, December 17

The cops are at it again. No, not the lights. This time they gave Jeremy a ticket for driving without his headlights on when it was just barely raining. Can you believe it? Right before Christmas! His face was all red like Santa or just like Dad's does when he gets angry. And he was so happy a couple days ago because he just got his drivers license. I don't know why he was so happy to be driving Dad's old blue station wagon when he's been driving the big dump truck and the front end loader for a long time. Who cares about some stupid car, I want to ride up in the air and make all that dirt spill in a big pile. Dad's already let me move the levers and turn the steering wheel when I was a baby sitting in his lap. I love the noises and how the motor makes me shake and feel tingly all over. Jeremy still likes the wagon better and says he isn't scared of no cops. He went out again tonight and Dad was smiling the whole time he was reading his lawyer papers.

Sunday, December 25

I hate going to church on Christmas because it's always so crowded. It's not like a regular Sunday when the church is maybe half full and we get a whole row to ourselves. We go every week and sometimes on Saturday evening during Christmastime because Dad is busy selling trees on Sunday. A lot of people bought trees this year, I think because they know about our Emdo problem and want to help out in some small way. Dad always tells them if they really want to help out they should stop watching the idiot box and start paying attention to the government and vote out crooked bums like Mr. Mahler. Dad talks a lot to God too. He's been praying more and more since our farm was condemned two years ago but things haven't got any better. He stays late after mass is over by himself or sometimes with Mom while me and Jeremy wait in the back. Jeremy teases me sometimes by flicking holy water on me. When Dad and Mom come back, their eyes are watery too but I think it's because they were crying and they don't want us to see it.

Monday, January 30

Last night was the first big snow of the year. A whole foot! I like it when everything's quiet and white in the morning and the snow's still falling and there's no cars on Matlers Lane. It's like the whole world's still in bed! Mom puts on the radio and we listen to the closings, mainly to hear if the courts will be open. They weren't so Dad had the day off, but he couldn't relax because he was out all night making extra money plowing the roads for other towns and then he had to help Jeremy shovel out our drive. I bet other kids get excited when it snows and the radio says school is closed, but for me today is like any other day. I have to learn my lessons before I go out and play. I do math by the kerosene heater in the kitchen and sometimes I get a headache if I sit too close. Mom cooks on the stove hooked up to a big gas tank or sometimes she uses the gas grill on the back porch. I love cookouts in winter! We've got generators for electric we use most of the time because Dad says we've got to be ready for when they turn the power off.

Friday, February 3
I think Dad's going crazy. Today I saw him talking to the Christmas trees! I was up in my bedroom this afternoon when I heard his truck coming back from delivering the last load of mulch. I looked out the window and saw him walking away from the house and out into the field, all the way across to the trees. I couldn't figure out why. Nothing needed tending. We shook the snow off the branches days ago. He didn't even look at the trees at all. He just went up and down the rows waving his hands in the air every now and then. He was far away but I could still see his head moving like it does when he talks with our lady lawyer whenever she comes over. He stayed out there a whole half hour. It was already dark when he came in for dinner. I didn't say anything when we ate because I was scared of him getting mad at me for snooping. I hope he's all right.

Wednesday, February 22

I saw Dad in the Christmas trees again this afternoon. It was really cold today but he was out there way past dark and Mom had to call him in the same way she calls me in when I'm playing. We had spinach lasagna with the crunchy wavy ends and Mom asked him what he was doing and I was glad she did. Dad said he was just going for a walk to relax his mind from all the Emdo trouble and he forgot what time it was. I didn't say anything about seeing Dad talking when nobody else was around.

Monday, February 27

He did it again. This time he didn't come in when Mom called so she sent Jeremy out to get him. I watched from the porch while Jeremy's flashlight jiggled into the dark than jiggled back out. I ran back to the table just as they were coming in and when Dad sat down he didn't take off his coat and there were big stains on his knees. Mom asked if anything was wrong and he said he didn't want to talk about it in front of us kids so we ate lukewarm pea soup and didn't say a word the whole time.

10 pm — They're yelling downstairs right now but I don't know about what. I hate when they yell. I get sweaty and my heart feels all heavy and I wish I could run away but I'm stuck where I am. Don't listen. I'll press my ears closed hard and listen to the marching sounds in my head.

Monday, March 13

Mom and Dad yelled at each other this afternoon. Dad might have been angry over the court and how the judges always seem to see things Mr. Mahler's way. The judges are talking about only giving us a month before they give the order to evict us. That gets me scared too. Where are we going to go? I don't want to move to Pennsylvania. I like it here. Thinking about having to move always makes Dad super angry, but I don't think that's the reason they fought. I think it's because Mom caught him sneaking out to the Christmas trees this morning after he didn't go near them for two weeks. I heard him shouting things like I'LL DO WHAT I WANT! and then he went out there again tonight.

Thursday, March 16
This is the 4th day in a row Dad's gone out to the trees. He doesn't care who knows it anymore. Today when he came home from court he went straight there and didn't even bother to change. I followed him out there and he was on his knees again getting his good pants dirty. He had his hands folded like he was in church and he was saying thank you thank you thank you over and over again. He saw me and gave me a big hug and then we went back inside and he told us the judge gave us four more months. He said it's because God is hearing his prayers and granting more and more each day and pretty soon He'll fix it so we never have to give up the farm.

Sunday, March 19
We didn't go to church today. I was putting on my good shoes and my itchy church shirt when Mom came in and told me to put on my play clothes and boots. She had a funny look on her face and I didn't know what it meant until I got downstairs and Dad told us from now on we were going to have our own services out in the Christmas trees. He said he never felt closer to God then when he's praying in that grove and we should

know that same feeling ourselves. He said God listens there more than He ever did in church and His voice whispers back when the wind shakes the branches. When we got outside Dad had us repeat a prayer he made up while we stood in a circle holding hands. We didn't sing songs or have readings or shake each others hands like they do in church. We just listened to Dad pray out loud with our heads bowed. Sometimes he sounded all far away like our priest sometimes gets and that felt funny. I didn't want to be there. What if someone saw like Mr. Mahler? Jeremy was standing next to me and whenever Dad closed his eyes I looked up at him and he made cross-eyed faces back. That made me feel better until it was over. We were out there a half hour and all that time God didn't talk back once.

Sunday, April 16

Dad acted really strange at today's Easter prayer circle. He said God was talking to us right then and couldn't we hear Him or feel His power in our hands? All I felt was Jeremy tickling my palm with his finger.

The Land And Its Righteous Custodian Shall Not Be Parted.

Dad said these were God's exact words and he made us memorize them. That's when Jeremy let go and called everything the BS word and ran back into the house. He and Dad fought the whole rest of the day. Jeremy said hanging onto the farm was making Dad nuts and no piece of land was worth going crazy for, specially when the town offered twelve million dollars and he turned them down flat.

Dark Territories   *Neil Morris*

Monday, April 17
Jeremy ran away. He took the station wagon while everybody was still sleeping. Mom was upset Dad didn't call the cops but he said he didn't want the police to know our business because it will get back to Mr. Mahler. We got a call from Aunt Helen around 10 o'clock and she said Jeremy was safe with her but he wasn't coming back to the farm until Dad stopped acting crazy and being so stubborn. He said Dad should just take the money and be done with it and Dad got real mad when he heard that. He said he loved the farm so much all the money in the world couldn't make him give it up. The land wasn't for sale and neither was he. Dad called Mr. Mahler a word that sounded like whore, and whores couldn't understand that some things couldn't be bought, and if Jeremy didn't understand that then he was a whore too and shouldn't come back.

Sunday, April 23
Mom wouldn't pray with Dad because of what he said to Jeremy and she kept me from going too. She hasn't talked much to Dad since Jeremy left and Dad's been real busy doing double work loading and driving out the mulch. Pretty soon summer's coming and Dad will have to go out and fill pools on top of everything else. I wish I could help. I wish we were a farm again and we could grow things and Dad wouldn't have to do all these different jobs.

Sunday, May 7
GOD ANSWERED DAD'S PRAYERS! Dad called me and Mom outside and there was a big smile on his face for the first time in weeks. He said God had given him the power that would keep us on the land no matter what Mr. Mahler and all the cops in this county

did. God says Dad is the righteous custodian of the land and He's seen fit to make it so that Dad can't be taken away just like it says in those words we memorized. To prove it Dad told us to try and lift his leg off the ground. Mom said it was crazy but she pulled on one foot and I pulled on the other and wouldn't you know it we couldn't move them! I pulled so hard my hands turned white but Dad stayed stuck to the ground! He wasn't fighting back or using his muscles or anything. Then we tried it with him lying on his back and we only could spin him in circles. That was so cool! The last thing we did was try to dig the dirt from around him but the dirt kept spilling out of the shovel like it had a mind of its own and filled up the hole we just made. That was just too crazy!

Monday, July 10
BAD NEWS! The court says we have to get out by July 17th. That's next Monday. Our lawyers can't get us any more time and the judge expects us to be gone by 3 o'clock in the afternoon or else he'll order cops to take us away by force. Dad laughed at that, not because of the surprise he's got for them, but because the cops have to come from another town since the cops in this town are so crooked.

Sunday, July 16
Reporters and TV men came today plus neighbors from across Matlers Lane and a whole bunch of people who had the same Emdo thing happen to them. It was like a big party! There was a band playing on a truck trailer in the field but they played Mom and Dad's kind of music so I didn't like them too much. Everybody stood along Matlers Lane holding up big signs that had Eminent Domain Abuse written in a big red circle with

a line through it. Cars honked their horns and people cheered and everything was really fun. Then a priest led a prayer circle in the Christmas trees as the sun was setting but Dad still didn't say anything about his power. I heard the priest ask Dad why he hadn't packed anything up when he knew the town could take everything tomorrow. Dad just said it was all safe in God's hands.

11:30 pm — It's so hot and I can still hear people moving downstairs. I'm scared about tomorrow. I don't think I'll be able to sleep.

Monday, July 17
I'm amazed to say I'm writing this in our kitchen tonight. WE'RE STILL HERE! The cops didn't kick us out even though they were here all day. It looks like Dad's power scared the cops away but he said it's because there were too many TV cameras and people here for them to do something that would make them look bad. He said they will probably wait until everybody's gone then move in when nobody's looking. They are cowards.

10 pm — All the reporters and sign people went home. What's it going to be like if they do come tonight? Are they gonna have guns? Are they gonna break down the door? Are they gonna hurt Mom or Dad? Will we have to go to jail? All we want to do is live in our home and I can't see why we have to go to jail for that.

It's late but Mom and Dad let me stay up. They don't want me out of there sight. I jump every time I hear a sound outside. I think it's them coming.

Tuesday, July 18

No cops came last night but they showed up this morning and hung around again all day. Ever since we locked the door tonight all Mom and Dad do is sit on the couch and stare at it. All they had to eat was a bag of potato chips. Mom takes a nap every now and then but Dad's eyes never close. Mine don't want to close either.

Wednesday, July 19

I'm writing this from the kitchen of aunt Helen's house in North Wales Pennsylvania. Jeremy is here but we are not all together. EVERYTHING HAS GONE WRONG!

It all started when our lady lawyer called early this morning. We all jumped when Dad' phone rang. And I was just falling asleep too! After he hung up he told us the cops didn't come in because they were ordered not to. Instead the judge was so mad at us for refusing to leave he decided to fine us $5000 a day going back to Monday. Mom said that will take away from any money we get for the place and Dad just got real mad and said she's thinking like Jeremy. I've never seen him so mad. He called Mom a traitor to him and God if she didn't believe that the power He gave him would never let us lose the farm. Money didn't matter. Not when God was here to make everything all right. Mom screamed back Dad had really gone crazy and that was the last I heard before I ran outside and hid in the stable. Mom called for me a little later and she sounded so awful I had to answer. She was crying and she told me to get in the pickup. I asked her what about Dad and she said he would be out soon. I knew it was a lie and I wanted to run back inside and be with him, but I felt so sad for her I got in the truck anyway. We drove to Matlers Lane and the cops in the car at the side of the road looked at us then looked back at the house. LEAVE MY DAD ALONE! I screamed and I think I started to cry but I don't remember. The next thing I knew I woke up here.

Friday, July 21

We talk to Dad on the phone. Even Jeremy. Dad says he's sorry and he misses us but he can't leave. He hopes we understand and says we should pray for him. I don't know about anybody else but I do. I ask God to help him win but mainly to keep him safe. Dad told a reporter the day we left it didn't matter if Judge Hanley fined him $50,000 a day, he wasn't leaving. When the judge read that in the paper the next day that's exactly what he did. Dad says by his count he must owe about $115,000 by now. Mom laughed when she heard that. We took turns saying goodbye and I went first. Dad told me to be strong, to be Mom's little man and be ready because pretty soon I was going to feel the farm under my feet again. I said yes to everything and then I said I love you.

Monday, July 24

THOSE BASTARDS HURT DAD! They came when nobody was looking just like Dad said they would and they hurt him! The cops called here three hours ago and we haven't heard from anyone since. Mom's already left for home and Jeremy's been constantly calling back but he doesn't get any answer. Jeremy woke me up when they called around 7:30. Mom was freaking out and crying so much Jeremy had to take the phone. They said Dad got hurt bad in both his legs when they took him out of the house and they were rushing him to the hospital. They were just about to say where when there was a loud staticy noise and the phone hung up. Jeremy and me haven't been able to sit still ever since. I can barely write this. THEY DID IT! Mr. Mahler and the cops did something to Dad when they found out they couldn't move him! Aunt Helen's saying we should come in the living room and see what's on TV but I'm so mad I don't want to watch anything. Now she's yelling for us to come so I guess we have to go.

1pm — I CAN'T BELIEVE THIS IS HAPPENING! When I first saw the TV it looked like there was a war going on in a city with a mountain sitting in the middle of it but the words over the high up pictures said New Brunswick. That's the city close to where we live! Fires were burning and a big path went from the mountain all the way back to the river then past the river as far as you could see. Buildings and streets should have been where the path was but there was just crumbled houses and halfs of houses and lots of smashed cars. Fire trucks and police cars were everywhere and everything was covered in dust. The people talking over the pictures called the mountain an earthen formation and said there was a hospital buried under it.

Then they showed some pictures from earlier. Traffic cameras on Route 18 showed a giant wave made out of dirt instead of water spilling into the river then climbing back out. It ran over cars on the highway and plowed into the city. Next came more high up pictures of the path. Johnson Park. College buildings. People's homes. Everything got swept away. The helicopter flew all the way back to where the trail started and hovered over a giant pit cut in the ground like somebody cutting out a piece of cake.

When the pilot said he was over what's left of a farm I knew who that somebody was and what was going on. DEAR GOD, please forget the promise You made and save Dad and all the other people in that hospital! Make the land go away. Shovel it back into its hole.

Take care of everyone who's been hurt. Forget our stupid farm and help everyone who's lost their homes today.

5 pm — I was thinking God answered my prayers when the mountain fell away from the hospital. I hoped the landwave would go back to the farm but it moved farther away instead. More houses got crushed. More people are dying. When pictures of the empty looking hospital came on there was a feeling in my heart that Dad wasn't alive either. I don't know what made me feel that way but I wanted to cry so much. Only one tear came out because I stayed strong for him and the only reason the one got out was because I was mad at God. Madder then I am at Mr. Mahler. Mad and mixed up. How could God be so mean? Why didn't He keep Dad safe? Why won't He just make the landwave stop? Even as I write this the people on the TV say the landwave keeps moving to the south west. They say at the speed it's going it will be in Pennsylvania in six hours.

Tuesday, July 25

Last night the landwave stopped at the feet of its new custodian. It's not Mr. Mahler and it never will be. It's not Jeremy even though he's the oldest. It's not Uncle Mark or Aunt Helen. It's not even Mom who took care of Jeremy and me while Dad took care of the farm.

IT'S ME. THE LAND CAME TO ME. It found me even though the police moved us from aunt Helen's to a high school gym in another town. A lot of people were crowded inside and they were all scared of being swallowed up by the landwave. They all had the same look on their faces like Mom and Dad had when they waited that night for the cops. When the landwave came there was a rumble that shook the gym like thunder after lightning strikes real close to your house. Only this rumble got louder instead of fading away. Everybody screamed and started running for the doors but by the time they opened them the land was already coming in like grain out of the silo chute and pushing them back. I was afraid too but then I saw the first little stones and rocks come trickling out from under all those jammed together people. They rolled along the basketball floor right up to my feet and when the first piece touched my sneaker EVERYTHING STOPPED! The rumble ended and the land quit gushing through the door. Then the land made a path under my feet and I followed it with everybody else out to the parking lot where a huge land pile rose up so high it blocked out the night sky. Stars showed when the pile started to melt down and all the dirt spread over everything until it was about five inches deep. People got on their knees in all that fresh soil and started praying to God and thanking Him for saving there lives. I got on my knees too only I said a prayer for Dad and told God He still had a lot of explaining to do. Then I stood up and when I dusted off my knees I could of swore there was a piece of Christmas tree branch stuck to my pants.

What inspired "Excerpts From The Diary of Jared Hafler"?

Anybody familiar with Central Jersey news will instantly recognize the plight of the Halper family in Excerpts From the Diary of Jared Hafler. Concluding with the eviction from their farm in the summer of 2006, the Halpers spent nearly ten years bitterly fighting eminent domain proceedings initiated by the township of Piscataway. City officials condemned the property under nebulous legal definitions regarding the evidence of "blight", and vowed to preserve the acreage as a public park. Whether or not they will break their promise and sell the land to a wealthy developer remains to be seen, but given the level of corruption in the case — corruption that disgraced an advisor to former governor James McGreevey — the odds are pretty good expensive condos or a shopping center will occupy that space one day. All in all, you can't get any more New Jersey than that.

Cat & Mouse
William Mingin

Bill Mingin has published 18 short stories, with more forthcoming; one was reprinted in The Year's Best Fantasy 3 *(Hartwell and Cramer), and five others were given honorable mention in* The Year's Best Fantasy and Horror. *He's also published over 200 reviews, essays, and articles; he currently reviews for* Strange Horizons *and* AudioFile Magazine. *He's a graduate of Clarion West (2000), is married, and runs a small book-export business.*

*A*s Danny huddled on the steps of a church near the graveyard, crying and trembling, it seemed impossible that something so strange, so bad, could have started with such a small deviation from the norm: a single bag lady in Dartwood.

There can't be a bag lady here, he'd thought as he walked down Liberty Street under a canopy of old trees, their leaves bright in the autumn sun. Not in Dartwood, the picture-perfect northern New Jersey suburb, where streams of men and women with briefcases took the train to NYC early every morning, newspapers under their arms, and returned at dusk to dinners pre-stocked by chefs-for-hire. Where children wore white sneakers that never got dirty, because Xbox games didn't dirty them; teenagers had stock portfolios; and everyone got a foreign car at 17. Where on fall weekends Dads raked leaves for fun, the real work done by short Mexicans during the week, and Moms cooked as a hobby.

Couldn't be. That's what made it so strange to see one.

Her flesh was white and creviced and thin, almost crumbly-looking, like dry dough, but under each arm a wad of flesh bobbity-obbitied as she poked through a trash can. Thinking the word "strange" made a chill climb his back, like a delicate spider.

He started when someone called, "Danny!"

It was Billy, coming up behind him, grinning slyly around a smoke dangling from his lip, as if he'd heard a new gross joke or had a magazine rolled up under his jacket, and he'd open it and say, "Did you ever see anything that big? Can you believe those?" But he just kept sauntering up, and Danny fell in beside him.

"What's up?" Danny said. Billy didn't say anything or look at him. He just kept smiling and walking. The old woman was wearing a garbage bag like a shawl; it looked like she'd just climbed out of the trash and was looking for something she'd dropped, maybe a valuable can of cat food not quite emptied. As they came up she stopped and stood still. She didn't look at either of them. The sun, nearing west, flushed her dour face, like a corpse on fire.

"Don't look at her," Billy said out of the side of his mouth.

"What?" Danny said, turning back to look.

"Goddamn it," Billy hissed, "what'd I just say?" As they moved away she began to forage once again. Billy, continuing to walk, said softly, "When's the last time you saw a bag lady in Dartwood?"

The question made the spiders dance on Danny's spine.

"Yeah," said Billy when he didn't answer. "Me neither. Well, today I saw five. In Dartwood. Investment banker capital of the northeast. Major crop: lawn. *Bag ladies.*"

"Where we going?"

"Your place. Your parents are away, right?"

They were away, so they popped two beers. Billy sat on the kitchen table, where Danny still didn't dare sit, though he was almost old enough to drive. Billy rested his shoes on the back of a chair, drank, and smoked. He was the perfect combination for getting away with what he shouldn't: dressed and acted like a retro hood (black leather, tee shirts, unfiltered smokes), thought like a hard-line Republican, and treated adults like an ambassador negotiating valuable mining rights with a nation of simple-minded, hot-tempered savages.

Today his tee shirt was one they were selling at the gag gift shop at the mall: "Crocodile Hunters Do It With Heart," over a picture of the late Steve Erwin.

"It's not natural," Billy said, swigging beer from the can. "Something's going on."

Now monkeys, who had been eating ice pops, swung on Danny's spine as if it were a Maypole.

"What do you mean?"

"Five bag ladies appear on the same day in downtown Dartwood, where the police don't even like it if black people stop to ask directions? Where the cable company doesn't carry *Univision*? Where Spam is considered an ethnic food? That's what I mean."

"Well—what do you think they're doing here? Who are they?"

"Plants!"

"Plants? Like *Day of the Triffids*?"

Billy exhaled smoke and gave him a puzzled look.

"You know, the old movie—-man-eating alien plants that tried to take over the earth—"

Billy grimaced. "No, jerk-off. Not that kind of plants. Spies—moles—phony bag ladies slipped in by liberal do-gooders. They did something like that out in California a while back. Some town outlawed people sleeping in the streets, so all these do-gooders came in and started laying around. It started a big stink, the news covered it, and the law got repealed. O'Reilly gave it a slam."

"There hasn't been any problem like that here."

"Just my point. The Dartwood police keep the bums *out*. So these liberal pussies come in dressed as bag ladies, see? They get arrested, and next thing you know, every paper in the country's got a story about how Mrs. So-and-So who teaches sociology at Whassamatta U. got roughed and cuffed in Dartwood, she gets interviewed on 'Good Morning, America', and 'Doonesbury' shows the citizens of Dartwood sending the local cops to train with the Taliban. The town council doesn't know whether to shit or wind its watch, and they repeal every anti-vagrant law on the books."

"Sounds farfetched to me."

"Right, right. You think they're man-eating plants. Much more reasonable. We should sing them some Slim Whitman and see if their heads explode."

"Well at least I don't think pinkos have sent their grandmothers to infiltrate Dartwood. Jeez, Billy. Next you're going to tell me the CIA has your breakfast cereal bugged."

"Why should they? I hate poor people and minorities, too, just like the government! But this is some kind of plot." He furrowed his brows. "A terrorist cell?"

"Of old ladies?"

"The terrorists use women now. There could be anything under all that stuff they wear. Those outfits are like garbage burkhas."

"They're not covering their faces," Danny pointed out reasonably.

"Whatever." Billy swigged, puffed, and looked thoughtful. "Anyway, whoever they are, we're the only ones who've noticed."

"So? What're we supposed to do?"

"Expose them! For the honor and glory of Dartwood."

"Expose bag ladies? Gross! Anyway, what do you care about the honor and glory of Dartwood?"

"Nothing. But think how cool we'll look if we're the ones who foil the plot. Especially if it turns out they're dangerous."

"Let the cops get them. Why haven't they, your precious don't-even-like-blacks-asking-directions cops?"

"Probably no bag ladies down by the Dunkin Donuts. No, don't you see, that's just more evidence for my theory. If they were real bag ladies, the cops would have hauled them in by now. They haven't, so either, A, they've been paid off, or B, they know the scam and they're ignoring them to avoid a confrontation. Unless, of course, they've clouded their minds—can man-eating plants do that?" He smirked around his beer.

Danny ignored the dig. "I can't wait until your weird brain gets unleashed on the adult world. So what do you want to do?"

"We start slow. We stalk one, follow her until she's out alone someplace—"

One of Danny's eyebrows went up. "And then we expose her?"

"Yeah, then we confront her, tell her we've seen through her disguise—"

"I don't want to see through her disguise!"

"Bite me. We give her a good scare and find out who's behind this. C'mon. What've we got to lose?"

Danny sighed, resigning himself. "All right, all right. Let's go."

*

They'd found their bag lady, a fat one with lank silver hair who swayed far to either side with each step. She wore dark green trash bags over a tattered black dress and a holey sweater, and on her feet black rubbers lined with more green plastic and bound with rubber bands. Billy leaned over to Danny and whispered, "She's probably wearing the rubbers so she won't get AIDS." When she was upwind a scent like damp magazines in the basement drifted toward them on the crisp fall air. They followed her down Torrance Street past the cemetery fence, toward Dartwood Park. A policeman stood near the park entrance in the shine of a streetlamp still pale in the dusk, idly releasing and then catching a nightstick that hung from his wrist on a strap. He was there to keep kids like them out of the park at night.

As the old woman came near, though she still swayed, she seemed to scurry on tiptoe, like a mouse in a cartoon; she was through the light and past the cop more quickly than seemed possible. The cop didn't seem to notice her.

"Dartwood cops are even stupider than I thought," Billy muttered as they approached.

"Or she *did* cloud his mind," Danny answered, feeling the old chills return.

Rather than skulk they simply strolled by, nodding slightly to the policeman. He watched them as they passed, letting them know he was aware of them.

"Us he sees," Billy muttered again. "Jerk."

Once around the corner, they slipped over the low iron fence into the park, and by cutting across a lawn, came to a path a few hundred feet behind the bag lady without being seen.

"Perfect!" Billy whispered.

Now, away from the street and the cop, they began to close on her. She stopped, and as if by reflex, Danny and Billy stopped, too. Though well into dusk, it was light enough for them to see a cat running down a cross path with the funny little fast-motion movement cats make when hurrying but not running full out. The bag lady swooped—there was no other word for it—down on the cat, her rags and bags billowing out around her like bat wings. She lifted it up before it could even cry out and tore its head off, a shower of blood pattering on her bags like rain. Grinning, she lifted the body of the animal over her head by its tail and swallowed it whole, her jaw gaping huge, her outline slithering as her flesh expanded to envelop her meal, like a snake's elastic body, so that she appeared not human but some other kind of creature with human features plastered over her skin. She swallowed the body quickly and tossed the head in one of her bags, like saving the best tidbit for later.

Danny and Billy went cold and rigid. Then Danny threw up, everything he'd ever eaten, it seemed, gagging out of him in a rush. Only fear and Billy tugging at him frantically got him to run, blindly, tears in his eyes, acrid vomit in his throat and nose. He didn't look back, he couldn't, but Billy did.

They came out of the park across from the church. They tried to get in, but it was locked and they had to stop for a minute because Danny was sick again and had to sit. "Oh, Jesus!" he said, whimpering, his face down on his arms, his arms on his knees.

"Don't think about it," Billy said, urgent, pleading.

"She saw us?" Danny asked, raising his tearstained face. "You sure she saw us?"

Billy cursed himself for blurting it out. "I don't know. I think so."

Then they both noticed dim shapes in the near-dark, as if at random, here and there on the street in either direction, not looking at them, but between them and any houses, people, help

"What are they?" Danny whispered. "Where did they come from?"

"I don't know. Can you walk? We've got to try for your house. Come on." Billy pulled Danny up.

As if in answer to this motion the women moved in, almost floating, old and shrunken or layered with fat, wrapped in plastic, patches of cloth, ill-fitting shifts, holding string-handled bags. One wore a torn coat over the remnants of a man's suit, another, an old robe bound up with so many layers of plastic and paper, she seemed a shabby, many-petalled flower. They moved slowly, shuffling, hobbling in the moonlight, their legs, where exposed, dirty, sore-ridden, and scarred, their faces so wrinkled they looked inside out. Some of them were grim and their eyes gleamed, but others smiled, as if they were going to ask for quarters and say, "Bless you."

Billy pulled Danny forward. Danny, his eyes wide at the women's shambling approach, began to scream.

"Come on," Billy shouted and he dragged Danny after him, toward one side of the narrowing circle. They ran for a gap and Billy thrust Danny ahead. Danny got free. Something large swooped near his head, but he ducked and kept going. "Run!" Billy yelled, "Run! Don't stop!" Danny ran. He didn't stop, but he looked back once. Billy had stumbled when pushing him forward, but hadn't fallen. He was held up by the bag ladies.

*

Danny didn't know how long he lay on the living room floor after he threw himself inside the house and bolted the door. He wasn't unconscious, really, but in a kind of daze, where he couldn't move or act. Then he finally rolled over and stood, bleary and confused, like a drunk. He fell into a chair and sat there crying and shaking for a long time.

He could get to a train, maybe, keep going as far as it would take him. What would happen to his parents? And the rest of the town? *I'll be alive*, a voice in him said; *I'll be alive. Maybe once I'm away I can get hold of my parents, warn them. They'll think I'm crazy. But I'll be away from the old women. I'll be alive.*

But what about Billy, who had pushed him ahead, who had let them catch him so that he, Danny, could get away? Was there any possibility that he was still alive? That he wasn't like— He thought of the cat and threw up bile into a potted plant.

But what if the cop had come by, and heard Danny screaming? Maybe Billy had been saved, those things scared away. It could have happened. *I've got to find out*, he thought. *I can't just leave him, without knowing what happened. I have to see if I can help him.*

It was that knowledge that he trembled against, straining not to know it. *I've got to go after him. If I can get him away, once we're out of here, maybe we can warn people.* If there were two of them, it would be easier to get people to listen.

He stood, still trembling, then slowly went up the stairs to his parents' bedroom and took the .38 out of the nightstand near the bed. He flicked off the safety the way he'd been taught in the Police Firearms Safety Course and walked back down the stairs.

At the door he hesitated again, all parts of him at war, then put the gun in his jacket pocket, where he held it, and went out.

*

He went back to the street where they'd taken Billy. Down near the cemetery something shone white in the gutter, under a streetlight.

A jawless skull.

Billy, he thought, his eyes filling with tears, but then he saw something just beyond it on the sidewalk and after a few seconds recognized it as a splintered billy club.

They got the cop, he thought. *He won't report in, they'll look for him, they'll find the bones, there'll be an investigation. So no matter what happens, they'll find out. They'll find a way to kill them.*

Beyond the club lay other bones, picked clean, blue-white in the moon- and streetlight. Over near the cemetery fence gleamed a brass button. He scrambled over the black iron fence, as they did every Mischief Night, and pulled out the gun.

As if waiting for him to cross that boundary, they rose up from the shadows, like the dead on Judgment Day, pale in the moonlight, smelling of damp and dead things, unspeaking. Beyond them, he could see that some of the graves had been disturbed. He began to tremble, submerged panic and horror rising up to drown his thinking in gore. A squat, waddling woman stepped out from the ring, in closer to him, and he whined involuntarily, like an animal, no more aware of the gun in his hand than he was of the position of the moon.

She stared at him like a fat-throated frog with black and glittering chicken's eyes. He could not help but watch as she parted the black cloth of her dress. Her fat breasts hung loose like a pair of old men's faces. She hooked a finger in her navel and pulled outward. It had to be skin pulling back, like a pouch, but it opened like a mailbox. Then he realized *that* was the mouth, in what he'd thought was the belly. The features on her face suddenly seemed a mere pattern, like the spots on a toad.

Despite himself, he had to look into the opening, the dark inside, and there in the gaping space lay a small, crumpled thing, a broken baby, but the limbs were too big, and then he saw it had Billy's face, pinched and agonized, the limbs crumpled and splintered as if he had been forced into a hatbox. He had to be dead. But the face, eyes still closed, puckered further, as if sensing someone else's presence, and started crying. One of the hands reached out toward him, as if asking to be drawn out.

"Billy," he said, weeping, and took that hand—
with the masters in huge ships of light, moving
endlessly through black space
hunting in the ship's depths, feeding on vermin
the ship screaming through atmosphere, a crashing
and tearing
fearful and confused—this world was strange—
angry, abandoned, no one to tend to them—lonely
hunted, burned, hanged
hiding in shadows—in the cities—never staying in
one place too long—eating the unmoving ones stored in
the earth, when there was nothing else
then taken up into the blessed white spaces, rooms
hard and artificial, like the ships, once again fed and
cared for
and sometimes late at night the caretakers lying
atop them, caressing them—some they swallowed
entire, but not often, because they were fed, and the
taste brought back hard times
then thrown into the cold streets, abandoned
again—no food but what could be found—anger again,
hunger so painful—the taste of people better with
hatred—warm blood, thick flesh, crunching bone, but
also memories, fear, all the electricity within them
the policeman screaming as they pulled red things
from inside him and ate them—and a glowing image, a
little boy, a piece of his past, came out, too—absorbing
that, swallowing it all down, and then the rest of him
and then some of the hard parts came back out
Danny knew all this in a moment, through that
touch, though he was touching *Billy's* hand, pulling at
Billy, but he wasn't coming—
Then an image came to him, some Discovery
Channel show where a tropical fish swam near a reef,
raising an imitation insect on a kind of antenna, bait for

its prey, but not a real creature, just a part of itself, an appendage, like its own tongue

and he knew that he was touching *her*

And Billy, whimpering, pulled at him, and then Danny brought the gun around and shot, two, three times into what had perhaps been Billy, watching the force of the bullets absorbed, even the energy of their sound sucked in so that before it had reached the edges of the cemetery it had stopped, and he realized the energy of the bullets was feeding her, too. Perhaps Billy, if not already dead, was dead now, but Danny's hand was caught in something sticky, and he was being pulled in to be his twin. The gun fell from his nerveless hand and he screamed, screamed again, his scream dwindling, swallowed up, as if he were falling—

*

An insomniac walking past the cemetery in Dartwood—where it was, after all, safe to walk at any time—glanced in surprise at a squat, unwashed woman in rags as she passed by him. A strange sound came from her, as if large pretzels were snapping beneath her dirty robes. He was afraid if he looked at her too closely, she would ask him for money, so he looked the other way and kept on walking.

What inspired "Cat & Mouse"?

There's an unfortunate human tendency to consider people different from ourselves—especially people with something "wrong" about them—as actually alien, as if they weren't really just other people. And when they're alien, they become frightening. This story makes that real, with appropriate consequences.

In the sf I've read, sometimes there isn't enough about the small, complicated, gritty details of life: trash disposal, can openers, minor skin ailments, silly names for pets. What if there were vermin—and vermin control problems—on generation ships? And what if, instead of intelligent/wise/scary aliens, all that was left after a crash were the cats or ferrets? Only of a kind that was very, very alien?

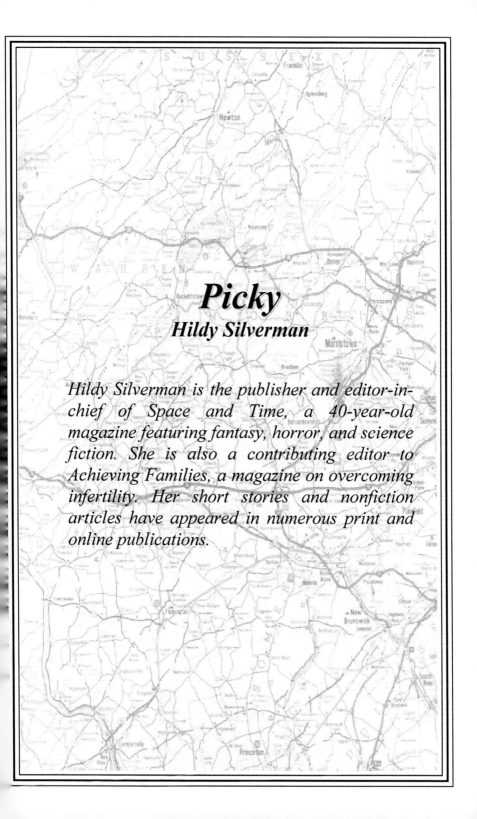

Picky
Hildy Silverman

Hildy Silverman is the publisher and editor-in-chief of Space and Time, a 40-year-old magazine featuring fantasy, horror, and science fiction. She is also a contributing editor to Achieving Families, a magazine on overcoming infertility. Her short stories and nonfiction articles have appeared in numerous print and online publications.

*T*hree years old, and Sarah still wouldn't eat.

She'd nibble. She'd pick. But actually consume? Not once since she'd been weaned. Food was her arch foe; mealtimes a battleground. It was her parents only source of aggravation with their otherwise model child.

"Time for me to go back to work." Mommy put down a spoonful of peas and picked up the Courier News. A few weeks later, she had a much-less stressful job than mommying at Lucent Technologies.

Sarah's parents put their own ad in the Courier News and interviewed potential nannies. One named Mala told them, "I raised five of my own. I'll get the princess over her fussing." Then Mala flashed her teeth at Sarah, who giggled. Mommy and Daddy were sold, and it became Nanny Mala's job to make 'choo-choos' out of unwanted spoonfuls of peas.

After they left for work, Sarah played with her bunny, Bunny, while Mala watched people fight over baby daddies on T.V. When Sarah got bored, she tugged on Mala's skirt.

Mala put her in her room. There Sarah played with her toy piano and didn't come out again *like-a-good-girl-or-else*.

Mala let Sarah out at lunchtime. Sarah climbed into her booster seat and told Mala an important story about Bunny's garden of magic planted things. Eating them made Bunny super-strong.

Mala put Sarah's plate in front of her. Its three compartments were filled with yogurt, cut up hot dog, and chunks of yellow cheese. Just looking at them made Sarah tired.

"Hurry up." Mala stuck a fork in a hot dog slice and squished Sarah's fist around it. "It's almost nap time."

"No, thank you, please." Sarah wanted to show off her good manners. She wanted Mala to start liking her. Mala smacked Sarah's hand.

Sarah's eyes filled up with wet. So did her mouth. "I said, eat. Now!"

She must've used her manners really wrong. Sarah didn't dare say anything else.

Mala slapped her hand again. Twice. The back turned red like Snow White's cheeks. "I don't care what kind of crap your mamma puts up with. When *I* say eat, you eat."

Sarah's stomach rumbled. She listened to it, but, as usual, had no idea what it wanted.

Mala tapped her foot. Sarah picked up a piece of hot dog and licked it. It tasted like floor.

Her cheek stung before she even saw Mala's hand fly. *"Eat it, you spoiled brat!"* A slap matched each word. When the words stopped, the slaps continued.

Sarah made her eyes follow Mala's hand. As soon as it got close, Sarah turned her head and bit down on Mala's finger. Sweet and salty flowed into Sarah's mouth. For the first time since she'd stopped sucking on Mommy's boobies, Sarah *tasted.*

Mala screamed. She pushed Sarah's head with her other hand and yelled bad words, until her finger snapped off between Sarah's teeth.

Sarah's tummy roared and woke up her taste buds. She tried to chew slowly, to make it last, but couldn't. She tongued the soft and chomped the crunchy and slurped the juicy.

"Sweet Jesus!" Mala fell down and hugged her hand. She squealed and rolled around like a piggy in mud. Sarah giggled. She didn't know Mala could be so funny.

Sarah slid out of her booster seat. She scrunched down next to Mala's face. It had turned a weird gray color, but she still smelled so very yummy.

"Can I have some more?" Sarah remembered her manners. "Please thank you?"

But she was too hungry to wait for an answer.

What inspired "Picky"?

This is going to sound awful, but my little story was inspired by my own darling little girl. She has always been a picky eater and, Jewish mamma that I am, her fussy eating habits often drive me to distraction. In this case, distraction begat a short fable, speculation on just what it might take to get her to stop picking and start chowing down.

Poppet
Kathryn Ptacek

Kathryn Ptacek was raised in Albuquerque, New Mexico and received her B.A. in Journalism from the University of New Mexico. She has published a number of novels and short stories in many different genres, as well as numerous articles and reviews. She is also the editor of the critically acclaimed Women of Darkness *and its companion* Women of Darkness II *(both Tor), and* Women of the West *(Doubleday). She edits the monthly newsletter for the Horror Writers Association and is the publisher/editor of* The Gila Queen's Guide to Markets, *a market newsletter now in its 20th year. She lives in Newton NJ with three demonic kittens and the ghost of her late husband Charles Grant.*

*T*he fourteen-year-old kid across the street plays the trumpet. He plays every day and sometimes at night, always rather enthusiastically, if not particularly well, although he's much better now than four years ago.

Right this moment he is belting out "Louie, Louie." I've never heard that song performed with a solitary brass instrument, and I hope I never hear that rendition again. Some things just aren't meant to be.

He debuted with "When the Saints Go Marching In," got stuck on "Heart and Soul" for a year or two, and has just recently progressed to the Russian folk song, "Meadowland," and some old rock classics, among them "Blue Suede Shoes" and "Peggy Sue." It is to his credit, though, that I do recognize all these tunes.

Each day he intrudes into my life a little with that golden trumpet. Even in the winter with our windows closed and his windows shut we can hear the music faintly, as if from a great distance. If only we were that lucky. But we're not, and the kid and his folks still live close by, and when it comes springtime, their windows fly up at the first hint of good weather, as do ours, to catch those wonderfully warm and fragrant spring breezes, and it's time once more for young John Philip Sousa to perform before his captive audience. The kid has even been known to even play the trumpet at night—after eleven, and sometimes after midnight on weekends. Never for very long, though, and no one except me seems to comment on it.

Sometimes when the kid sees that I'm home or sees me passing the window either upstairs or downstairs, he whips out the ol' trumpet and starts in. Sometimes he hangs out his window and toots it in our direction, and I have wondered what would happen if he slipped just the tiniest. Sometimes he stands in their kitchen which faces our house, or on the back porch and practices those songs. Sometimes I wish I were Artemis, the Divine Archer with a conveniently handy bow, and a magic arrow to shoot that way.

The kid sees me, and somehow senses that I hate that, that I hate to be watched in my very own house, and he smiles, and I realize then how very small and close and pig-like are his dark eyes. And again he raises the trumpet to his lips.

Sometimes when I lay down in the bedroom for a nap, I think he must be telepathic, because the instant I curl up on the bed, the trumpet begins. And I imagine those pig-like eyes with their dark intent. I complain a lot about young JPS to my husband, who smiles rather patiently. He doesn't have to listen to the kid all day long in the summer. My husband works at an office and commutes those long hours from our small northwestern New Jersey town to the city, New York City, that is, and often he's traveling in other states on company business.

I, on the other hand, don't work, or that's the opinion of those who are forever calling me during the day or dropping by "just to chat." Just because the women and men in this neighborhood aren't sure about me, doesn't mean they avoid me—after all, gossip can't operate in a vacuum, and they have to have something to fuel their talk.

Of course, I work, although not in an office. I have many important things to do. I have this wonderful house—a large Victorian with ten rooms all of which exude dust constantly—which always needs cleaning, no matter how hard I work at it—and a truly immense yard with numerous azaleas and rhododendrons and honeysuckle and lilacs and wisteria, and over a dozen flowering trees as well as those that bear fruit.

And I have a huge garden—with rosemary and rhubarb, sunflowers and sage, larkspur and lily of the valley, hensbane and hemlock, mint and marigolds, leeks and lavender (both English and French), borage and basil and bay leaves, daisies and dill and daffodils, cabbage and carnations, poppies and potatoes, three kinds of lettuce as well as endive, radishes and roses, carrots and caraway, sweetpeas and spinach, string beans and bush beans, Halloween pumpkins and colorful squash—and all these plants need to be attended on a daily basis.

Some people garden; I GARDEN. In some ways it is my life, and I guess my neighbors think I'm a little dotty on the subject. They tend to their little patches and are quite complacent about the matter. On the other hand, I yell at the kids who look like they might even be thinking about approaching my garden, and I have been known to turn the hose on a dog or two.

I'm sure the moment any new people move into the neighborhood, one of the older residents self-righteously takes it upon him- or herself to scurry on over there to alert the newcomers to just what sort of place they've gotten themselves into.

It's all a matter of coincidence, of course, but no resident of the house on our immediate right stays there longer than a year or two.

Sheer happenstance.

And it's true that the crows and marauding squirrels and gophers leave my garden alone. Not even the bunnies are so bold as to nibble there.

Happenstance again, I tell you.

On our left is a narrow street, hardly more than a car and a half wide lane. The house where the boy with the trumpet lives is on the other side of that road.

It's not that far away; not more than a stone's throw, not more than the blast of a trumpet. So, I listen to the trumpet as I trot from room to room, and not even the growl of the vacuum cleaner, not even the blaring of the CD player, not even my own off-key humming can totally shut out the efforts of our young would-be musician. Not even earplugs work one hundred per cent. I know because one day I tried them out of desperation. Somehow, the trumpet always manages to wheeze its way pass them.

So I do my work—the many chores about the house—and then it's time for the fun stuff, the labors of love out in my yard. I open the back door and go past the twigs of ash hanging over the door post and walk outside. I like to prune my dozen roses and admire the tender blossoms as they unfold from tiny tight buds; I like to watch a small seedling grow minutely each day, unfolding bit by bit so that it finally stands straight and tall in the nurturing sun and starts to bear fruit. I even like to weed, although I don't have many stragglers to pull from the soil. I really enjoy this. I thrive on my gardening. I talk to my plants and sing to them, and not even the trumpet music seems to deter them.

I know the kid's piggy eyes are upon me as I stoop and stand, then bend down to inspect my long-stemmed flowers. I know he watches, and I do not like that. He has altogether too much free time. He needs to be kept busy, I tell myself, and wish his mother would send him to camp. Boot camp, perhaps.

But of course, she doesn't, and he continues to watch me each day I wander through my garden, picking the sugar snap beans or strawberries, harvesting the zucchini which flourishes so well, or snipping off a dead leaf here and there, or admiring my berry bushes.

He watches, and I wait, and within moments he begins playing.

I glance up at his window, and he is looking down at me, his eyes unreadable from this distance. He continues to play, the music somehow louder than a moment before. Such strong lungs, I think. I pick up my basket filled with the harvest and go back inside to wash the produce.

In the evening I return to the garden to examine the herbal portion of my garden. They are so pretty these plants, with their lavender flowers and white spikes, tiny crimson and emerald petals and silver striations. I like to touch them, stroke the soft stems. In a way, they are my friends.

I look up, and even though it is dusk, I see the kid staring at me. Doesn't he ever read, or watch TV, or play video games like the other kids around here? It's not healthy for a boy of his age to always be looking out the window at his neighbor. I wait, but he doesn't play the trumpet. I shrug, take out my shears and clip off a handful of herbs and head for the house. I am no sooner in the kitchen than the trumpet begins.

The curious thing about the kid—one point, that is—is I've never heard him play the scales. And I always thought that was such a significant part of learning to play any musical instrument. My mistake, I suppose. And he never really plays anything long enough—he flits from song to song, day in, day out. He should concentrate on one song at a time, I think, but then I'm no musician.

I hum to myself as I wash the herbs, and realize the tune is "Stars and Stripes Forever," which the kid has just recently been learning. I know because whenever he plays it, I briskly snap my fingers, trying to get him to quicken the timing. He doesn't count very well, does the kid. What a shame. That's the true mark of a good musician. Ah well, I never said he was good, not yet anyway.

I dry the herbs carefully and spread them on a clean linen towel in the sunshine. How pretty are the leaves. In one cupboard I reach past the jar of alfalfa—it's supposed to keep the home safe from poverty and hunger—to get the other jars with the beans in them, and the one with the dried material well behind those.

I take out a handful of the castor beans from the glass jar on my counter and admire them. So pretty in their shiny casings, and such a dreadful oil that comes from them. I shake my head over that mystery.

The mix from the cupboard is a combination of dried leaves and flowers of datura, also known as Jimsonweed, the Ghost Flower (no doubt because of its white trumpet-like blossom), or Witches' Thimble. Datura doesn't grow here, but I have a friend in the southwest, who has the same interests as mine, and we exchange various plants that don't fare well in our own particular states.

The periwinkle I wash carefully, because I don't want to harm the delicate light blue flower. Its folk names are Devil's Eye or Sorcerer's Violet; I prefer the nickname of Joy on the Ground.

I take the anise leaves and inhale their fragrance, even before I crush them. I love anise-flavored candies and cookies. Its Latin name is Pimpinella anisum, but that sounds so silly. I use anise a lot at Christmas when I make dozens of cookies for various charities.

Then I take out the mortar and pestle—a beautiful grey and black swirled marble so cool to my fingertips even in the summer—and place them on the counter, then reach for the large wooden bowl needed for enchanting the herbs. I like the pattern in this wood and sometimes I take it in my hands and stroke the whorls, almost like those of a fingerprint. Perhaps it matches my own.

I go into the living room to collect a few items, and I see him standing on their kitchen stoop and he is staring across at the house, at me. There is only one faint light on in my living room, yet I know he can see me as plainly as if it were daytime. I cannot see his expression, because it is dark and there is a light on in the kitchen behind him. But I know that he is smiling. For a moment neither one of us moves, then he raises the trumpet to his lips. "Taps" this time.

Next I sit at the dining room table and spread out the plain white paper and the expensive colored pens I brought in from the other room and begin drawing. I hear the kid switch over to "Meadowland." Its such a nice song, and one of my favorites, and I can almost forgive him anything for that. Almost. He doesn't seem to quite have the soul for it, but I imagine that will come in time. He's still rather young.

The outline takes form quickly, and then I pay special attention to the trumpet in its hand. That's very important, you know. I draw in the features as best I can, making those eyes particularly piggy.

With my gardening shears, the green liquid of the herbs still on the blades, I cut out the shape.

It's a poppet, what some make from roots, potatoes, lead, bark or cloth. I prefer to make my out of paper; I have more artistic adroitness than sewing ability, and when sewing I somehow always manage to stab myself with the needle, and then the blood gets onto the material and spoils the poppet. No, far easier to use paper.

I smile at the poppet, satisfied with its resemblance, and go back into the kitchen. I grind the castor beans with my pestle, and sprinkle in some dried datura and pulverize that. Next comes the anise to join in the mixture.

Carefully I wind the periwinkle around the poppet's neck; what a pretty necklace it makes.

I pour the dried mixture into my wooden bowl, and take from the refrigerator a fresh lime. I don't grow them—it's not tropical enough here, so those just purchased from the local supermarket will have to suffice—and I slice it in half, then squeeze some of its juice into the mixture. I follow that with garlic buds in the garlic press, and watch as the smelly liquid drips into the bowl.

Again, I hum as I mash the ingredients together. I lean back because the odor rising from the bowl chokes me a bit and makes my eyes smart.

I'm not a violent sort, anyone will tell you that. After all, I live in a small town amidst the peaceful countryside, not in the large city with its rage and pain and brutality and stupidity. There are quite reasonable solutions to everyday problems, ends other than death, and God knows I've been tolerant enough so far. But there does come a time when you can only take so much.

He's playing "The Battle Hymn of the Republic." I hum along.

Then I retrieve a small artist's brush of natural camel hair and dip it into my rank brew, and smear the dark-colored matter onto the poppet's face.

I hear the trumpet stop abruptly, and the kid across the street screams. And then his mother is screaming.

I smile.

I don't much like the trumpet playing, but I know I'll get used to it, and he is improving, after all. But it's those damned pig-like eyes that disturb me the most.

I hear the rise and fall of the ambulance's wail as it rushes toward to our street.

The mixture is drying, and now I hold a lit match to it, and watch as the paper browns and curls and ignites.

The ambulance arrives; the attendants scurry inside the unlocked door.

I pour the remaining mixture down the sink and wash the bowl and mortar and pestle and put them back until I need them again.

The ambulance attendants bring a writhing form out on a stretcher; I am constantly amazed at how quickly these local volunteers can respond to an emergency. It's very encouraging.

The kid's mother is sobbing, and climbs into the ambulance with the others.

The poppet is now just ash, and I wipe it off the counter and into the trash bag. I wipe the counter clean; my kitchen bright and spotless, no doubt the envy of every suburbanite on the block.

I watch as the ambulance wails away into the early evening. The hospital is not far from us, not more than a mile or two, so I know the kid will get fast, if not effective, treatment.

And after all, blind musicians, I've heard, can be very successful. Just as long as the kid continues to practice.

What inspired "Poppet"?

Many years ago, Charlie had driven up to NECon in Rhode Island, while I decided to stay home and write. I didn't know if the new project would be another novel or a short story; I just knew I wanted to work on something. At that time, we had neighbors with an obnoxious son, who often practiced his trumpet at 3 a.m.—leaning out the window all the while. So, that day in July, with the windows wide open because of the New Jersey heat and humidity, I stared out into the backyard, my fingers poised over the computer keyboard as I waited for ... what? Divine inspiration? Something! Right then, the kid across the street began playing "The Saints Go Marching In" on his trumpet, and in that very moment the story unfolded in my head, and I started typing.

Man of Principle
Michael Penncavage

During the day, Michael Penncavage is a finance manager for an internationally recognized company. During the off hours, he has been an Associate Editor for Space and Time Magazine as well as the editor of the fiction anthology, Tales From a Darker State. *Fiction of his can be found in approximately 50 magazines and anthologies from 3 different countries such as Alfred Hitchcock Mystery Magazine in the US, Here and Now in England, and Crime Factory in Australia. One of his stories, "The Converts," is currently being filmed as a movie for release this fall. He is a member of the Mystery Writers of America, Horror Writers of America, and the Garden State Horror Writers.*

I always considered myself a man of principle.

But times like these really tried my patience.

Earlier in the day the temperature had climbed to a hundred and two. Tack on the humidity, it felt like a hundred and ten. Now, I'm no stranger to heat - no stranger to humidity. I've sat ten rows from the racetrack at Bristol Speedway where the heat coming off the blacktop supercharged the air to well over 120 degrees. I've had jobs that made me sweat it out under the hot Georgia sun while the ticks and the harvest bugs drained me dry.

But I've come to learn that Elizabeth, New Jersey, is no Georgia.

The house's lone air conditioner, located in the living room, had been chugging at maximum force for the better part of the day, but all the damn thing seemed to accomplish was cool a floor-mat sized space in front of it.

The rest of house hovered between being an oven and a furnace and stank of poodle and old lady. I'd lost count of how many shirts I'd sweated through during the day. Far more than I would have back in Kennasaw.

But hell - at least I had my beer.

Suddenly, the house began to shake. If I had not been living in this rat-hole for a couple of days I would have thought a storm was in the works, coming in off the Atlantic, maybe even putting an end to the heat.

But it was no thunder.

A Boeing 767 was coming in for its decent at Newark International Airport.

My empties started to w*rinkle* and *tinkle* on the kitchen counter as the plane roared overhead. Plugging my ears with my index fingers, I waited patiently until it passed. A moment later I began to smell the jet fuel drifting in through the window.

Lord, how I hated it here.

A shout from outside on the street seized my attention. Even though it was dark, there were enough streetlights to make it feel like day.

Three teenage boys passed by on the sidewalk. One of them held a radio and the music, rap, was blasting to a rhythmic *boom, boom, boom*. They were all drinking from brown paper bags.

Obviously, it was not a school night.

One of them, his bottle empty, decided the front lawn would make an ideal garbage can. I watched as he tossed it onto the ten-foot patch of green without a second thought. For a moment I considered going outside and reminding them that littering was punishable offense. I quickly decided against it as cooler heads prevailed. It was far too hot, and I had far more important things to worry about.

Sitting back in the kitchen chair, I glanced at the wall clock that had pictures of cats for the hours. 10:17PM - a quarter past the calico. My patience was starting to run out.

I wondered how it was in Georgia right now. Probably 75 degrees. A cool westerly breeze coming in off Texas, ensuring the temperature would be tolerable. Slight humidity. *No smog*.

Soon enough, I thought. The GMC Sierra was in the driveway, fueled and ready to go. The truck seemed as anxious as I to get back on the road.

With my gloved hand I took hold of the ceramic mug that read, *World's Best Grandma* and spat some chewing tobacco juice into it. Leaving Kennesaw, I knew I'd been forgetting something. A hundred miles up Route 95 I realized my pouch of dip had been left on my dining room table. Here, even the most expensive brand smelled and tasted like cow's ass.

A Gold Honda suddenly came into view. It slowed before signaling and entering the narrow driveway directly across from my house. I watched as the driver maneuvered the thin strip of pavement with barely a foot of room on each side. The license plate passed under a street light. Recognizing the letters, I knew I had my man. Charlie Palmer had *finally* decided to come home. I watched as a short balding man dressed in a three-piece heaved himself from the vehicle.

Finishing my beer, I stood up, tucked in my shirt, and checked my shin for reassurance. I was just about to step away from the window when a black Lincoln came into view.

It had been traveling fast, and the wheels released a soft squeal as the driver braked hard to make the turn into the driveway. Technique didn't seem to be much of a concern however as the car was thrown into Park with half the Lincoln still hanging out over the sidewalk.

There weren't suppose to be any Lincolns showing up tonight.

Problem.

All four doors of the sedan opened in unison. Four men stepped out. Four Louisville Sluggers came into view. None of them looked like they had been playing ball.

Big Problem.

This was *supposed* to be easy, not complicated. For a moment I contemplated going outside. The little voice in my head suddenly gave his opinion. Not going outside *would* be easier. However, this was a matter of principle.

And I *am* a man of principle.

I looked into the pantry. The 10 gauge was there, nestled snugly between the flour and Rice Krispies. I decided against the weapon. It wouldn't be necessary.

I strode through the kitchen, down the hallway, and out the side entrance.

By the time I had gotten outside, Charlie was already surrounded. Walking across the street, I was able to get a better look of what was happening.

Now, I don't much consider myself a racist or a bigot. I know enough of them but I don't much cotton to being one myself. But looking at the four guys encircling Charlie, I would be hard pressed to find a group of Italians looking more... Italian. All of them were sporting brand spanking new white tank tops. Between the chains, bracelets, and rings, there was enough gold on Charlie's front lawn to make Mr. T jealous.

"What seems to be the problem here?"

The one closest turned to me. "Who the fuck are you?" He was an ugly son-of-a-bitch, who had a wide, fat nose, sunken jowls, and teeth that would make some dentist a rich man. Obviously, no stranger to getting his ass kicked.

I supposed one more time wouldn't matter much.

"This here is personal business between Charlie and us." He held the bat at me in an intimidating way.

I supposed that was my cue to leave.

A second one turned to me. Enough tufts of hair were sprouting from beneath his shirt to make me wonder if he was wearing a sweater beneath. "Listen, Bayou Billy. If you know what is good for you, you'd better get out of here."

Bayou Billy?

While Fat Nose and Hairy glared at me, the other two kept Charlie from running. I glanced the surrounding homes to see if any lights had been turned on. I wasn't surprised to find darkened windows.

"Afraid I can't do that."

Even in the shadows I could see Fat Nose's eyes grow wide and the veins surface on his neck. Obviously his previous beatings had not taught him much. Taking a step forward, he swung.

I crouched down and the bat *whooshed* over me. While he recovered from the home-run swing, my leg shot out and the side of Fat's knee was introduced to my boot's heel. A *pop* sounded through the night air as Fat Nose's leg bent in a way it wasn't meant to. He collapsed to the ground, screaming in agony. Concerned the wails might prompt unnecessary phone calls, I planted four knuckles. Skin tore and bones broke as my fist reduced Fat Nose to Unconscious-Pulped-Nose. With anyone else I'd have felt bad about banging them up that way, but with Fat Nose my punch was probably going to improve his looks.

Hairy was next. I used the cushion of the grass to roll away and Hairy's bat missed me by a distance he should have been ashamed.

Yanking the Louisville slugger from Fat's clutch, I spun and swung at where I imagined Hairy to be standing. However, just like Fat Nose, I swung a little too energetically. The bat struck Hairy across his right temple with such an impact the Slugger splintered in two.

Hairy was dead before his body hit the lawn.

That upset me.

It was a shame to waste such a good bat.

The remaining two stepped up to the plate. The one to my left, a scrawny bastard with far too much grease in his hair, glared at me. "You just bought yourself a world of trouble, fella." The one on my right, after getting a good look at Hairy, looked less certain.

I spat out the remainder of my wad onto the ground. The nasty, cow's-ass flavor was beginning to make me nauseous.

Greasy and Uncertain suddenly grew backbones and charged, thinking they would be able to overwhelm me.

Mistake.

Thirty seconds later, I was standing over two more bodies.

Amateurs.

Charlie was standing in the same spot. Even in the dark I could tell he was sweating so profusely I could have wrung him on a washboard.

"Thank you for you help," he wheezed.

I dropped the remainder of Fat's bat onto the lawn.

"I see you've made plenty of new friends since moving to New York, Charlie."

He looked at me questionably. "I'm sorry. Do I know you?"

I looked down at the bodies strewn about the lawn. "You haven't learned from past mistakes, have you?"

"You came out of Mrs. Furloff's house. Are you her son?"

"The Poodle lady?" I shook my head. "No. No relation."

"Then what were you doing in her house?"

I dismissed the question. "Let's talk about someone we both know. Remember Sam Speetwell?"

A look of recognition surfaced on his clammy face.

"You hightailed it out of Vegas with half million of Speetwell's money. You didn't think he would just let bygones be bygones?"

"If it's money you want…"

"Mr. Speetwell is paying me plenty, Charlie. I wouldn't have bothered coming all the way from Georgia if he wasn't." I reached down and pulled the knife out from inside my boot.

"Now hold on a minute! You're here to kill me?"

"Afraid so."

"Even after you killed *them*?"

"I couldn't have a group of lowlifes, Mob or not, bludgeon you to death and have everyone think I was responsible for such shoddy work. Sorry, Charlie. Nothing personal."

He tried to voice another objection. I was in no mood to listen. Not when there was 900 miles of road needed to be driven.

The knife passed quickly and cleanly through his jugular. Clutching his neck as if it would do some good, he stared at me wild-eyed before flopping onto his stomach. I hesitate to say he didn't feel anything, but it was a lot less painful than going out under a hail of baseball bats.

A lot more professional.

After all, I am a man of principle.

What inspired "Man of Principle"?

There really wasn't anything specific that inspired this story.

All That You Can't Leave Behind

Harrison Howe

Harrison Howe has sold over 80 short stories and poems to various online and print publications. He is a past secretary and vice president of the GSHW. He edited the group's second anthology, Dark Notes From NJ, *in 2005. He also authored two ebooks, a humor book titled* Purring Elephants and Killer Coconuts *(Renaissance Books, 2006) and a poetry collection,* The Voice of Your Brother's Blood: Crying *(eTreasures Publishing, 2006). He is editing the forthcoming anthology* Darkness on the Edge: Tales Inspired by the Songs of Bruce Springsteen, *to be published by PS Publishing in 2009.*

*T*he air in the crowded gymnasium is thick with cigarette smoke and too many unrealized dreams and I burst out the side doors into the cool night, gasping.

I'd half-expected it was going to be this bad.

The air out here, though far less restrictive than that inside, is still stale. It seems the entire town—one I have not visited since my departure twenty years before, not even waiting for my diploma to arrive in the mail but getting on the bus while the crepe paper was still flapping on the bleachers where the graduating class had sat—is draped with the same cloying atmosphere. The whole town? Shit, the whole *state*. I feel like I'm choking being back here. On the horizon I can see industrial buildings and gray smoke against the darkening sky, planes going to and from Newark Airport lifting into and gliding out of gray clouds. Like one I had arrived in myself just fourteen hours ago; the familiar sight of cars moving along the Turnpike and the industrial buildings heaving smog into the air as I sank closer to the earth clenched my gut. Even at 10,000 feet. I was home. I had not wanted to feel that way but there was no denying it. I'd spent eighteen years clawing my way out, and not even Mary Jane could keep me here.

What's worse, I see *her* everywhere.

Despite the urge to run I stay put, one hand on the cool bricks, my tie loosened and askew, champagne stains on my shirt. We'd toasted to ourselves just thirty minutes ago, a hundred-and-thirty arms raising stemmed glasses in salute to I don't know what: our glorious pasts? Our futures? It all seemed so trite, somehow. Like we were still a bunch of adolescents who were going to walk out of that gymnasium and set the world on its ear. But most never walked further than across the Turnpike to labor like my old man in the smoke-spewing factories. It's almost funny to hear the star running back still reveling in his three-touchdown, hundred-and-ninety-eight yard playoff performance, or the class valedictorian still quoting sections of her graduation speech. We're all just middle-aged bodies wrapped around the boys and girls we used to be.

I've gotten too many jealous glances from those who stayed behind, who built their lives in the shadow of this high school, driving home from work and maybe occasionally swinging by the old building, passing by the track field where they set records that have since been broken, or looking up at the window where they had sat in geometry class, acing every test. Most of them seem reluctant, or afraid, to approach me. Like they think I'm somehow better than they are, or that I think I am. They believe I stole away from this place and found success waiting for me like a pot o' gold at the end of a rainbow, but the truth is I've written far too many unsung lyrics that amount to nothing more than emotional vomit and I've gone days with nothing but loose change rattling around in my pockets and I've just about prostituted myself to every agent and record company executive I could get close to, with nothing to show for it but one lousy song on the debut album of some no-name band that sold just about three thousand copies. What I got paid for it took care of my rent for three months, and you'd be hard-pressed to find a copy even in the discount racks in the back of second-hand music stores.

But I'd come back to face the damned ghosts; they've haunted me for two decades and my plan of forgetting the past, moving across the country and churning out songs to let out the pain has pretty much evaporated and I've come home to lay all this shit to rest. I didn't even come back when my old man died; maybe I should have. But he wasn't the only ghost rattling in my head, and when I got the invitation to my high school reunion I figured, what the fuck? Maybe now was the time to put it all to bed. I checked off the box next to Will Be Attending and dropped it in the mail. Hell, I think now, I might even get a song or two out of it all, and immediately feel like a shit for thinking that. A shit...and even more of a failure than I already do. I could get a hundred songs out of tonight; it'll just be a hundred pages added to the drawer of songs that's ever-growing in the filing cabinet in my rented storage shed.

When dreams die, they die hard and stay dead.

There's applause from the gymnasium; it drifts out to me like the smoke from the stacks on the far side of the highway, like the planes bound for faraway places slipping into the sky. My God, they sound so happy; they've gotten stuck here, working like their fathers, and they're happy. Out here, I am miserable. Jesus, I wanted tonight to be about shutting up the ghosts but instead I've simply re-opened all the old wounds, ghost-fingers digging down deep into the raw flesh. I can even feel my father's beer-breath on the back of my neck.

I saw Mary Jane the first time at the edge of the parking lot when I got out of the taxi that dropped me here from the hotel a few miles away (I'd always dreamed of showing up at this gig in a limo, oozing success, a model on my arm, my blue-collar ex-classmates in their rented tuxes gawking); again by the table where the 1986 yearbook lay open; once more at a back table, face partially obscured by the centerpiece balloons. I looked her up in the yearbook, finger touching her smiling face. LUVYOU DONNIE 4EVR

& EVR glared at me like an epitaph from beneath her picture. I almost hurled the book across the room but someone I only vaguely recognized stepped up, grabbed my limp hand with his work-hardened, dry fingers and said, "Donnie Malin! Holy fuck didn't think I'd see *you* here!" Grinning like a fool and sloshing beer over the rim of his glass, the ghost of his adolescent aspirations floating behind his stare.

I take several gulps of the cool air, drinking it like I'd done the dry champagne just half an hour before, and just when I think I've gotten my nerve up to go back inside I decide to take a walk.

*

I caught Mary Jane's eye in the second all those graduation caps hung suspended over us, in the seconds after Principal Kurick had celebrated the ceremonial handing-out of those empty diploma folders and the second before gravity did its job, and she looked so excited and sad at the same time, and before I could mouth "I love you", which I intended to do, all that flat black and red cardboard with tassels trailing behind like comet tails came crashing down around us.

I realized that even then I had decided I would be heading to the West Coast with that guitar my mother had bought me for my twelfth birthday on my back and pages of song notes in my duffel bag. Set the world on its ear, hell; I was going to set in on friggin' *fire*.

If I had known about the baby, just a speck inside Mary Jane's young body, it wouldn't have made a difference. I had bought the bus ticket a week ago.

*

I walk across the teacher's parking lot in back, across the track field, around the bleachers where we'd sat all those years ago. The walk is as familiar as the strings on my guitar. Two decades of denial has done nothing; I am home.

She is there, the light of the moon and the night wind in her hair. She has not changed. God Jesus, so little has actually changed. I feel like nothing more than a ghost myself as I approach her. I don't know if I half-expected to find her out here. It's where I remember her most clearly: it was in the shadow of these bleachers where I believe the baby was made, in the cool grass at the edge of the old wooden bleachers. Not twenty feet from where we'd sit just six weeks later, tossing our caps into the air, me catching her eye, never having the chance to mouth those words I should have said, needed to say, the words that should have kept me here and all this from happening. Maybe it's that regret that's drawn me here.

No…it's more than that. I wonder if I'd be standing out here if I had a string of Billboard hits under my belt.

She's sitting on the bleachers, in the spot she sat on our graduation night, and rises when I get close. The gaping wounds twist like pale snakes around her wrists. I don't want to look at them, those ugly gashes only reminders of my guilt, but I look anyway. Shit.

"I was wrong, you know," I say. My voice in my ears is as alien as the sound of my footsteps in the empty halls of the high school, as alien as being in the shadows of industrial buildings so many I knew had wound up toiling away in. I hadn't even been able to resist driving by the old house, almost grounding my molars to dust as I sat at the curb, hearing my father's drunken outbursts behind the sun-faded walls. "Maybe I shouldn't have pushed you away, pushed aside what you wanted just to go after my own—"

She hushes me, raising a finger in front of my face. I want to feel her finger on my lips but I can't. At that moment I would chuck everything—every fantasy of playing at a crowded Continental Arena, every vision of my striding onstage to accept my Grammy award, every song lyric I'd ever jotted down—just to feel that finger on my face.

"We made our choices," she says, and looks down at her self-infliction. She had wanted to marry, to raise kids; kiss me off to work every morning and home at the end of the day, wash the factory stink out of my work clothes, make my lunch and pack it in an Igloo cooler, watch TV movies, visit our families on Sundays. "We both got out...in our ways."

Maybe...but it's been two decades and I've chased the dream long after it was dead, maybe I didn't make it but I did a lot more than anyone else back in that damned gymnasium...so why do I feel like a coward? Why do I feel like...like one of them? *Because you are*, my father mutters in my ear, so real I can feel the breath that pushes the words from his mouth drift past my earlobe. Maybe my old man was a miserable fuck but at least he was honest with himself, knew what he was; dragged himself off to work every day to keep a roof over our heads. Jesus, now *that* took balls. Did people really look at me like I was so fucking brave?

Twenty years and I'm still chasing that damned dream, playing bar gigs on weekends, working a forty-hour job at Tower Records, the time spent writing songs dwindling more and more. I spend a lot of time at work looking at the new releases and the magazines, seeing who made the cover of *Rolling Stone* this month. Mary Jane and my unborn child are gone and the factories are still spilling soot into the clouds and my father's blood still moves under my skin and most of the graduating class of 1986 has taken up after their retired or dead fathers and nothing's changed.

I've let the dream slip away, the reasons I ran out as dead as the look I remember in my father's eyes. The hollowed stare. I can't even look at her, look at my feet instead. One of my many unrecorded songs, the morbidly titled "In the Stench of Decayed Dreams", comes to mind (*Razor blades on wrists, shaking enraged fists/Who among us has not sobbed at the graveside of their dead dreams?*). Thinking of it gives me the courage to look up, to look in her face and tell her how sorry I am.

But when I lift my eyes she's gone. I can only see the gray smoke churning out of the smokestacks, so dark against the sky. My own enraged fists simply tremble at my sides.

*

So I go back into the gymnasium. Some of the helium balloons have begun to die, drifting near the floor. Others have slipped the ribbons that bound them to the centerpieces and are stirring up in the rafters. The band plays on; it's a group of seniors here from the school calling themselves The Chase. They aren't half bad. I think maybe they have a future, if they want. If they *want*.

And there is Allie Dunbarton, alone at a table near the musicians. I go over and she smiles, a crooked smile because one side of her face is mostly gone. She'd driven her car into a tree just a few weeks after graduation, leaving a note taped to her bedroom mirror that said she couldn't stand the thought of living the rest of her life here in this shithole town and didn't see any avenues of escape except the one she had chosen. I heard rumors that her father would come home from work smelling like factory fumes and touch her with his greasy hands, but who knew? There were a lot of rumors in a small town like this. She'd been a star in high school: cheerleader, honor roll, all that stuff. One of the most popular girls in the school. When the realization that that was over hit her, she hurled herself into that tree.

We all got out, in our ways...

She would not have given me the time of day all those years ago, but I ask her to dance and she says yes, and I lead her out onto the dance floor. For a moment we are alone out there, and then others make their way out to us. Some have factory-callused hands and that same tired blank stare my father looked at the world with; the rest are gaping wrists and fatal head wounds and one sad mousy girl I don't even recognize with the noose still trailing around her neck, and I think that after all these years I am not hardly removed from the life I had been so afraid to fall into, the life I had tried so hard to avoid. Part of me wishes I had had the balls to follow Allie Dunbarton's lead, or at the very least my old man's. That there's bravery in the life he lead hits me with a certainty that very nearly doubles me over. My God, the courage it must take to get out of bed and drag yourself through the factory gates day in and day out just so the kids who fear you and sometimes hate you can eat and have new shoes when school starts in the fall.

In our last phone conversation just two days before she cut her wrists, Mary Jane had said: *I think you're so brave, Donnie, doing what you're doing. New Jersey's no place for what you want to do. You're going where you need to go. I hope you find what it is you're looking for.* Sounding like what she was: alone and scared and pregnant. I was two thousand miles away, in a cheap hotel room, another thousand miles away from a future I needed so badly to get to, and how was I to know the future was the same as the past, black as coal?

I look into the eyes of all those around me, more and more drifting from their places at the linen-covered tables, looking for Mary Jane again, but I don't see her. It's just me and the rest of the brazen souls, those brave enough to do what had to be done, to play the cards they got dealt and keep playing even after they got beat over and over again, and those brave enough to fold when they realized they were losing the game and losing it big, and as I spin Allie Dunbarton through the crowd I can't take my eyes off them, the wounded dead and the lifeless living. I am part of them. I am home.

What inspired All That You Can't Leave Behind"?

The lure of the past has always been a theme I return to in my fiction; the idea that what we were always haunting our present selves. As high school is often a painful time for most of us, that purgatory between childhood and growing up complete with rejection, uncertainty and the longing urge to somehow fit in, I have used that time period for a few of my stories and found myself returning to it for "All That You Can't Leave Behind." Having attended school in New Jersey, I found it easy to place the story there: a grown up Donnie Malin returns to the Garden State for his high school reunion and faces all the ghosts—one in particular—that are dredged up as the place stirs memories he'd most like to leave forgotten.

The Crew

Gary Frank is the author of *Forever Will You Suffer*, a supernatural, time-shifting tale of unrequited love gone horribly wrong. He is also the author of a number of short stories, including "Stay Here", which received two Stoker recommendations, and was published in the 2005 Garden State Horror Writers anthology, *Dark Notes From New Jersey*. A member of the Horror Writers Association since 2005, Gary has also been a member of the Garden State Horror Writers since 2003 where he is currently the President. When he's not spilling his imagination on the page or working the day job, he's playing guitar. His next novel, *Institutional Memory,* is due out from Medallion Press in the Fall of 2008. For more info, head over to www.authorgaryfrank.com.

Mary SanGiovanni received a Masters in Writing Popular Fiction from Seton Hall University in 2007. Her fiction has appeared in anthologies and magazines since 2001, including two GSHW anthologies, *Tales from a Darker State* and *Dark Notes from New Jersey*. Her first novel, *The Hollower*, came out in 2007 from Leisure Books. Her next novel, *Found You*, is due out in October, 2008, also from Leisure Books. She lives in New Jersey with her son. On the web, Mary can be found at www.marysangiovanni.com.

Steve C. Gilberts has been producing fine art since 1981. In 1995 he began displaying his work at science fiction and fantasy conventions. In 2003 he made the jump into professional horror illustration starting with Space and Time Magazine.

Steven and his lovely wife Becky live in a spooky Queen Ann cottage in a small Dunwich-esk village in Indiana. While hiding from the townsfolk, he concocts odd illustrations for numerous publications including Elder Signs Press, Bad Moon Books, and Cemetery Dance Magazine.

His work can be seen on the web at:
www.stevengilberts.com